ARAÑA AND
SPIDER-MAN
DARK TO

2099 MORROW

ALEX SEGURA

Los Angeles   New York

© 2023 MARVEL

First Edition, May 2023

10 9 8 7 6 5 4 3 2 1

FAC-004510-23076

Printed in the United States of America

This book is set in MrsEaves

Designed by Kurt D. Hartman

Library of Congress Cataloging-in-Publication Data on file.

ISBN 978-1-368-07900-6

Reinforced binding

Visit www.HyperionTeens.com and www.Marvel.com

For Guillermo and Lucia

Wait—you're kidding, right?"

Araña landed hard in front of the creature—half man, half dinosaur. She straightened the large goggles that covered her eyes and braced as the man-monster turned to face her. She stole a glance at the group of kids clustered in the far corner of the exhibit—a class of middle schoolers on a late-afternoon field trip. They probably hadn't expected to see their educational adventure derailed by a low-rent Lizard wannabe.

"Your name is . . . Stegron?" Araña said with a tilt of her head, trying her best to keep one eye on the kids behind the villain. "What does that even mean?"

The creature seemed to lurch forward, with deceptive speed. Araña barely managed to sidestep Stegron's arm—feeling a slight breeze as it sped past her legs.

"My name . . . is *Stegron!*" the monster howled, frustrated at missing Araña. "Where is Spider-Man? Why is he sending his sidekicks to do his work?"

Araña leapt back, her feet landing atop a giant *Brontosaurus* skeleton. She felt her weight disrupt the balance of the bony structure. This would not last long.

"C'mon, Spidey can't be everywhere, dino-grouch," Araña said. The words tumbled out fast, her nerves propelling the banter more than a desire to quip with a scaly terror that made her nightmares seem tame. "You're stuck with me—Araña, seventh most important Spider-Person in New York City. Them's the breaks, eh?"

Araña pushed down on the skeleton's head with her foot; a low, creaking sound grew louder as she put more pressure on. The dinosaur-man's eyes bulged as he realized what she was doing. While he watched the soon-to-be-dismantled exhibit, she made a slight movement with her head, motioning for the dozen or so kids to dart toward the bright red Exit sign.

"No, no, what are you doing?" Stegron moaned. He seemed hesitant now, scared. Araña had done her homework before arriving at the Museum of Natural History. "Get off . . . No! You'll destroy that precious creature . . . Stop that!"

But then he paused, spinning his reptilian head around to spot one of the kids making a break for the exit. With frightening speed, Stegron shot his tail out, knocking the kid backward. Araña winced at the *thud* the kid's head made as it hit the linoleum floor. She'd made a mistake, she realized. He'd picked up on her hint, and now these poor kids might pay the ultimate price.

"Hey, lay off those sprouts, dino-bust," Araña said, watching as Stegron turned back to face her, his mouth baring his sharp teeth. "I know it's me you want, not some schoolchildren."

"You overestimate your value, Spider-Girl," Stegron spat. "I want Spider-Man, not some dime-store knock-off. I also want what's rightfully mine—behind those doors."

Araña knew exactly what Stegron was talking about. The museum had just unveiled a new exhibit—one that was linked to one of the most advanced dinosaur research labs in the world. Stegron wasn't interested in animatronic dinos or fossils. He wanted the lab—he wanted access to the DNA samples the press had been harping on in the lead-up to the exhibit's launch. He wanted to upgrade himself, basically. Though, if you asked Araña, when it came to upgrading, Stegron had nowhere to go but up.

Vincent Stegron was a dino expert, she knew. Had studied them his entire life. To, like, a scary degree. It wasn't just a calling; it was a damn obsession. Guy loved these extinct creatures so much he injected their

DNA into himself, trying to replicate what happened to scientist Curt Connors. Y'know, the guy that also turned into a giant scaly monster? The Spider-Man villain known as the Lizard? Yeah. Weird role model. The experiment stuck, though, for better or worse— Vincent Stegron basically *became* a dinosaur. The transfusion turned his skin scaly and hard, and gave him strength and speed and the somewhat pointless power of controlling any nearby dinosaurs. Sadly, the power didn't seem to work on fossils. Araña smiled slightly as she watched the fallen kid pull himself up. All she had to do, she knew, was give the kids time to escape. Give them a chance to survive. Then she could handle this Savage Land flunky. But first, she'd need to distract him.

As she leapt from the giant fossilized creature, a thought crossed her mind. She was so *new* to this. Being a hero. Fighting villains. It felt so surreal. The way it all came together, too. One day, she was your average New York teen, wandering through her day-to-day. Now she was something else. Something more important.

She landed a few feet away from Stegron, blocking his path to the next hall and the lab that had what he craved.

She yelled, loud and clear. The time for subtlety was gone. "Hey, kids . . . *run!*"

Stegron hesitated for a moment as he watched his baker's dozen of hostages escape. She could almost read his mind as the thoughts whirred past. He knew what he wanted. But Araña got what she wanted, too. The kids were almost out of danger, and that would make this a win, no matter what.

As Stegron charged her, Araña jumped over him, sending a swift kick into his face. She watched his head snap back as she landed behind him. She stole a glance at the exit and saw the last kid had made it through, and they'd be in the safe hands of the police cordon outside. She let out a quick sigh of relief. Then Stegron's tail slammed into her midsection.

Ouch.

There was no instruction manual for super heroes. No handbook that walked you through your rogues' gallery or gave you Spider-Man's cell-phone number. She'd been on her own since she started. Well, almost.

Since her teacher died.

She pushed the thought to the back of her mind as she sidestepped another swing of Stegron's giant dinosaur tail. She instinctively grabbed it, tugging—hard. Stegron flipped backward, crashing into a nearby dinosaur egg exhibit. Araña watched as the faux dino eggs rolled down the museum's expansive halls and into another section of the building, near the lab. She couldn't hear much under the laundry list of profanities the disgruntled Stegron was spouting. As hard as this stuff was, Araña realized, she felt good. She was making a difference. Saving lives and protecting people who would've been helpless without her here to save them.

"Y'gotta watch that tail, Steggy—may I call you Steggy?" Araña said as she shot a strand of webbing up and watched it connect to the museum's high ceiling. "It's prone to making a mess in here."

She swung back toward the giant fossil *Brontosaurus* and felt a sharp pang as she crashed into it. She completed the arc of her swing and watched as the pieces crumbled down on Stegron, burying and immobilizing the cold-blooded villain, who was well into his twelfth stanza of insults or colorful phrases.

She landed on a nearby perch and watched as the dinosaur-man surrendered to the pile of fossils locking him in place. She let out a long sigh, the exhale pushing a strand of her brown hair back. She was tired.

"This gets easier, right?" she said, knowing she was talking to herself but wishing she was talking to someone else. Someone who knew what they were doing. Someone who could teach her the ropes and save her some of the pain and heartache that had become all too commonplace in her life.

But no one answered.

She pulled her goggles off and rubbed her eyes, secure in the knowledge that Stegron couldn't see her face from what seemed like a million miles below. She was doing okay, Araña told herself—even without help. She was holding her own against a real Spider-Man villain, she thought. She was saving people. She was a hero.

So what if he wasn't Sandman or the Green Goblin? Someone's gotta take them down, right? She felt a smile form across her face. She was doing it.

She stood up and looked down at the defeated baddie. She'd done something good. On her own. And she'd had fun doing it.

She swung on a strand of webbing, landing near the edge of the dinosaur exhibit. She heard sirens in the background. NYPD could take it from here, Araña thought as she made her way to the exit. She let herself feel good. Why not? This whole experience had been the definition of "crash course"—painful, shocking, disturbing. But she'd kept at it.

She felt a sharp New York breeze slap her face as she stepped out into the moonlight. In a series of scary, haunting, and danger-filled nights, tonight had been a good one.

Araña shot another strand of webbing toward the

Manhattan skyline and pulled herself up, letting the
winds and a New York evening propel her home to
Brooklyn. She let the good feeling coat her, pull her
in close—but she couldn't shake something else. Something deeper. A feeling that this wasn't a sign of good
things to come—but the last good thing she would find
for a while. Before things got really dark.

What if you hadn't been there to help, Araña?

Araña closed her eyes, wincing slightly, trying to
will the thought away.

She was almost successful.

CHAPTER 1

Move along, freak!"

The words jolted Anya Corazon from her daze. Her usual zombielike morning walk from her papi's car to her locker at Milton Summer High School in Fort Greene, Brooklyn, wasn't the kind of thing she had to think about. She just did it, weaving through couples making out in the hallways, pep-club kids putting up signs for the big fill-in-the-blank game, and freshmen wandering around like lost children. But today was different. Today was loud.

Someone was screaming *at* her.

She spun around, arms coiled, as if bracing for an epic battle only Anya herself knew was coming. She could feel her friend Lynn stiffen behind her, surprised by Anya's defensive reaction.

"Anya, what the—"

Before Lynn could finish her question, Anya pinpointed just where the guttural scream had come from: Derek Lopez, Milton Summer's own USDA-approved football-playing bruiser. As usual, he was trying to

barrel through anything or anyone that stood between
him and the exit. As the team's star tight end, Lopez
not only got to score points on the field; he could
do whatever the hell he wanted off it. Right now, he
wanted to get past Anya.

It was fitting for the less-than-stellar week Anya'd
been having. She'd totally flubbed a gymnastics move
at gym on Monday; she'd basically slept through a
chem test on Wednesday, incurring the wrath of
Mr. Rodriguez; and she'd stormed out of the house
after another argument with Papi on Thursday. It'd
been the usual stuff—Anya had been out late; he was
worried. She understood where he was coming from,
but she couldn't explain anything more. She hated it, yet
she had no choice. And now, this.

Lopez reached over Anya and grabbed Lynn's arm,
tugging her friend out of his path. Anya heard Lynn let
out a pained yelp as she tried to yank herself free. But
another sound accompanied it—a bass-like "Huh?!"
bursting from Lopez as he felt himself being pulled back.
He let Lynn go just as he was tossed into a nearby set
of lockers. The soft krnnch of his stocky body slamming
into the metal was kind of satisfying, Anya thought.

She didn't want to do this, but she would if she had
to. If there was one thing Anya couldn't tolerate, it

was a bully, and Lopez was the textbook definition of "bully."

Anya watched as Lopez rubbed his eyes, unable to believe that *anyone* could toss him around like that—much less *Anya*.

Anya felt Lynn behind her.

"Uh, girl—how did you do that?"

Anya watched as Lopez slid down to the ground, moaning slightly, his thick, steak-like hand resting on his forehead. She didn't want to feel good about this. She didn't like hurting people. But sometimes you have to stand up for yourself.

Before Lynn could press further, Anya spun around and motioned for her friend to follow her down the hall. They were late, and a small crowd was starting to form around the downed doofus. It was time to move.

Once they were out of earshot, Lynn didn't let up.

"Anya, seriously—you're maybe five feet tall and a hundred and ten pounds soaking wet," Lynn said, matching Anya's pace. "You just tossed our prime-time football hero into a wall. Like, how is that even—"

Before she could finish, the second bell clanged. They were officially late.

"Lynn, gotta run, okay?" Anya said. "We can talk more later."

Without another word, Anya pivoted down the school's C wing, leaving her friend to stare at her back.

Anya picked up as much speed as she could as she ran down the now-empty hallway. She didn't want to break into a full sprint—not for fear of getting caught or breaking a sweat, but because she was still figuring out how she worked.

And what she could do.

She wove into room C223 and managed to slide into her seat with only a dirty look from Mr. Rodriguez, their dapper chemistry teacher, who definitely gave off some Lestat vibes. As she placed her backpack on her chair, Anya glanced at her cell. There was a text from her papi, Gilberto.

You need to be home right after school, Arañita. Don't forget.

Anya rolled her eyes.

Why did everything have to be so complicated? Things had been so much simpler . . . before. Secrets made normal life so fraught. Still, the alternative was much worse. If Anya didn't safeguard her secrets, people could get hurt. Badly.

She let her heart rate slow down as she settled into her seat. She could still feel herself vibrating slightly from the encounter in the hallway. She needed to be better about things like that, needed to exert more control. Her head had been elsewhere, though.

She'd woken up that morning with a jolt, realizing she'd slept through her alarm. Her papi was already well into his own routine, too. He'd made a habit of reminding her that he was not responsible for her getting out of bed. She was old enough to set her own alarm. He was right. Anya was in high school—she had responsibilities, not just at school, but to her friends.

Anya managed to toss on some clothes and eat a waffle on the way to the bus, but she still hadn't felt like herself when she walked into the school lobby, and getting into a skirmish with a thickheaded jock definitely didn't help in that department. She unspooled her mental to-do list and shuddered. She needed to write up her story on last night's girls' softball game for the school paper, the *Lancer*, and she had to finish a paper for Ms. Dymond on Le Guin's *The Left Hand of Darkness*. There weren't enough hours in the day. Not anymore. Not since . . . it happened.

Her thoughts were derailed by sharp whispers behind her.

"Yo, bro—did you hear about this Spider-Woman?"

Anya felt her ears perk up at the exchange between the two boys seated behind her, Jesse and Dave. She leaned back a bit, watching Mr. Rodriguez scribble their assignment on the whiteboard, but tuning in to the hushed conversation happening behind her, straining to hear over the sounds of the classroom.

"Naw, naw, dude—she's a girl, a kid," Dave said. Anya could visualize the bespectacled boy shaking his head incredulously. "Well, no, maybe like us? Like our age? But no way she's an adult."

He almost spat out the last word, as if it were a profanity.

"So, what, she's, like, Spider-Girl?" Jesse said. "Spider-Teen?"

A pause. Anya caught Mr. Rodriguez glancing toward her and the boys before turning his attention to his work. She let out a brief sigh. A few seconds later, Dave hissed back at his friend.

"I think her name is Araña?" he said. "Or something like that?"

"Araña?" Jesse asked, his voice rising above a whisper for a moment. "The hell does that mean?"

Anya spun around, a sharp smirk on her face. If they were going to talk about her, she was going to make sure they talked about her *correctly*.

"It means 'spider,' boys," she said. "Try cracking a book open sometime, yeah?"

She saw them roll their eyes as she wheeled back around. She could make out bits and pieces of their continued gossiping as she pulled out her pencil and started jotting down notes. She had to focus on class.

She had to figure out a way to sneak away during her lunch break to finish that work. Anya Corazon had a lot to do. And yet, she couldn't fight back the smile that lingered on her face.

Sure, life was complicated. But it was also . . . kind of fun?

CHAPTER 2

Anya felt a pang of guilt as she watched Lynn looking around the school's front steps. After a few moments, her friend shrugged her shoulders and headed toward the bus, filing in behind some of their classmates for the journey home.

As the bus pulled away from the curb, Anya stepped out and made her way down the street toward her apartment.

She felt bad. She didn't like lying to her best friend, or her father. It wasn't who she thought she was. Yet over the past few weeks, she felt like she didn't have much of a choice. She felt lost—just floating without any guidance or direction. This was new to Anya, who had always prided herself on being independent and self-aware. But lately, she just didn't know what to do next. That was on a good day.

It all seemed so clear to her; at least it had a few months back. Anya was driven. Not just to be a good student, but propelled by information and experiences. She knew part of this behavior was from her dad, who'd built a reputation as one of the best investigative reporters in the city. It was probably why she felt so passionate about her own little corner of journalism at the school paper. But it was more than that. She wanted to make the most of what she had—academically, but also in terms of everything else she could take part in. Whether it was riding the bench on the girls' basketball team, doing design work on the yearbook staff, or cranking out stories for the school paper. She knew colleges looked at more than just your report card. They wanted to know potential students were "three-dimensional," and Anya was going to do whatever it took to take that leap. Her parents had been to college, she knew—but it had been a struggle. Her mother taking night classes while working and caring for a baby. Her dad going to community college while he worked as a stringer at a low-rent tabloid paper that paid him by the word. They'd scrounged and clawed for their education. She knew they had wanted more for her. It wasn't just about letting Papi down, either. It was about taking the opportunities presented to her to achieve the dream she wanted for herself. Anya wanted to make a difference. To help people. She wasn't sure what that entailed yet, exactly. Whether it meant being a reporter and following in her papi's footsteps, shedding light on the dark truths powerful people wanted to hide, or something more direct—like medicine or community organizing. But she had time to decide. She just needed to make sure she got her shot. The shot her parents had worked for her to get.

As Anya pulled onto her block, she felt her left hand instinctively move to her right arm, sliding under the sleeve of her shirt. She looked at the intricate tattoo that graced her skin. She touched the tattoo and felt it pulse slightly—she could feel it and see it. The tattoo seemed to tingle slightly—similar to what you'd feel if your arm or leg was asleep, but sharper. More . . . powerful?

She pulled her sleeve down with a jerk.

Anya always figured she'd get a tattoo one day. But she'd envisioned it as an operatic act of teen rebellion, in the wake of some mega-argument with Papi. She never expected to wake up one day with one etched into her skin. She also didn't expect to get spiderlike powers in the bargain, too.

To say it'd been a hectic few months would be an understatement.

Anya clutched at her neck, where the amulet her mother, Sofia, had given her had once hung. It'd been years since Anya had seen her mother, yet she could still remember her soothing voice, the smell of her skin, the kindness of her eyes. Sofia had left her—and

Gilberto—abruptly when Anya was barely a child. The reasons Sofia gave them were lost to Anya, memories that had faded and not been reinforced by fact or conversations with her father. Gilberto refused to speak of his wife's disappearance, only saying that Anya's mother was a good woman—and she had her reasons. Her absence had left a void Anya could never fill, despite her father's valiant efforts.

Gilberto was everything Anya could ever hope for in a father—responsible, caring, patient, and understanding. But she knew he felt the same pain she herself did. She wondered why her mother's absence stood between her and her father, a deep canyon neither would dare cross.

CHAPTER 3

It was that same curiosity that led Anya down the path she now found herself on. Just a few months back, she'd been wandering down the same street when she saw a figure pausing at her door—the woman looked older than the mother she remembered, but seemed so much like her, too. Anya remembered calling out, but before long, the woman was darting down the street.

Anya gave chase, barely keeping pace with the woman. They ended up in Fort Greene Park; the early evening had faded into the darkness of night, making it nearly impossible for Anya to keep tabs on the woman. Was it her mother? she wondered. Had she finally returned after years away? Anya dared not play with the possibility in her mind, but she could also not help herself. She wanted it to be true.

But the park was huge, and Anya soon found herself alone—standing before the massive Prison Ship Martyrs Monument, the white tower almost shining in the black night. The woman was gone, and Anya felt anger welling up inside her. Anger she'd kept bottled up for too long.

"Fine. Run," she said under her breath. "We were doing well enough without you anyway. We don't need you."

She opened her mouth to continue when she heard a loud crash—she turned to see a cloaked figure running toward the monument, panting heavily from the strain.

The cloaked figure stopped a few steps from Anya and pulled its hood back to reveal a man—clean-shaven, long brown hair, and dark, dangerous eyes. Under any other circumstances, Anya might have found him cute. But in an empty park in the middle of the night, her guard was way up.

"Hey, calm down, buddy," she said. "I've got a can of Mace in my pocket just waiting to explode on you."

The man raised a hand as if to silence her. She didn't like that.

"I said—"

"Please, be quiet," the man said, his voice cracking with desperation and what seemed like fear. "They'll find us."

"Who are you?" Anya whispered.

The man motioned for her to follow. Unsure why, she did. They sprinted around the monument, draping themselves in the shadows of the aging building. She watched as the man peeked around the edifice before turning back to Anya.

"My name is Miguel Legar," he said. "And I'm in quite a bit of trouble. So are you, unfortunately."

Anya didn't see the arrow so much as feel it speed past her, just a moment before it became embedded in the monument's stone base. She backed up, dizzy, as Miguel did the same.

"We have to go," he said.

He grabbed her hand, and they raced toward a thicket of trees, matching each other's steps. But there were other sounds cutting through the dark Brooklyn night—more footsteps, raised voices, and dark laughter.

"Why . . . why are they after you?" Anya asked between breaths as they made their way farther into the dense woods. "What do they want?"

"Me," Miguel said, unfazed by the sprint in a way that made Anya immediately jealous. "They want me. I'm part of an organization they want to see destroyed."

Anya let out a relieved breath as they reached a clearing, but it was short-lived. A shadowy figure stepped into the fading moonlight. The woman seemed to be in her thirties, with close-cropped blond hair and light blue eyes that shone through the night. But there was something else about her—something dangerous and timeless that let Anya know there was much more to her and to the four other women who stood by her side. They remained draped in darkness and shadow, but their eyes seemed to . . . shine?

"Miguel, how nice of you to crop up," the leader of the group of women said. "The Sisterhood was looking all over for you. And I see you've brought a little friend."

"I, uh, I just met him," Anya stammered. She hated herself for being afraid and found herself course-correcting immediately. "But y'all don't seem that friendly, no matter what you say. So why don't you leave Miguel here alone, and I won't have to call the cops?"

The leader turned to look at Anya for what seemed like the first time. She squinted her eyes slightly. Her faux-friendly smile morphed into an annoyed sneer.

"Anya Corazon," she said. "You have no idea what you're getting into."

"How—how did you know—"

Before Anya could finish the question, the women leapt at her and Miguel—revealing a bevy of weapons: swords, bows and arrows, and a bo staff. Anya and Miguel were soon surrounded. The two had their backs to each other, both in defensive stances.

"Anytime you want to suggest a quick, nonviolent way out of this, I'm all ears," Anya said.

She was joking, she knew, because she was frightened. She should be home—starting her next English paper, on *Absalom, Absalom!*—not getting jumped by a gang of female furies with deadly weapons. Why had she followed that woman? Anya wondered. Were they connected?

"Let me handle this," Miguel said, his voice low.

Anya turned to respond, but Miguel was already in the air—executing a backflip that sent him into the fray. Within seconds, he'd knocked two of the four attackers down, their weapons clattering to the ground. In another moment, only Miguel and the group's leader remained. Anya swallowed hard.

"You were always good with the fodder, Miguel," the woman said. "The finest Hunter of the Spider Society."

She stepped closer. Miguel seemed hypnotized by her movements—as if unable to avoid her stare. Anya stepped back slowly. She should run, she thought. Get home. Lock her door. Forget any of this happened. But she couldn't leave Miguel here—even if she'd just met him. *And what the heck is the Spider Society?*

"But I'm a Hunter, too, Miguel," the woman said. She was inches away from Miguel now, her face close to him. "Charlissa, of the Sisterhood of the Wasp. Perhaps the finest Hunter either group has seen . . ."

She turned away from the mesmerized Miguel, her eyes locking on Anya. Anya thought she'd stepped out of Charlissa's sight, had figured out a way to escape. But that was a lie. Charlissa had seen every step she'd taken.

". . . since Sofia Corazon."

Anya gasped.

The woman named Charlissa smiled. She straightened and walked a few steps toward Anya, Miguel still frozen. The other Sisterhood members were slowly getting up, recovering from their quick defeat at Miguel's hands. Anya felt her body lock in place, her eyes the only part of her she seemed able to move. Even blinking felt like a chore. Charlissa crouched down, that smug smile on her face.

"That's right, little one," she said, her voice melodic in its tone. "You didn't just stumble upon this moment. We brought you here. We know what Miguel is after— and we intend to stop him."

Charlissa's veiled threat was followed by a hollow *thunk*—and Anya took a few steps back as the leader of whatever the Sisterhood of the Wasps was toppled forward. Anya looked up to see Miguel, standing over Charlissa, a long, bo-like staff spinning in one hand.

"We have to go."

They ran.

Anya felt the branches and leaves brush and cut against her face as she and Miguel darted away, toward the park's edges, toward civilization. Anya felt her legs cramping. A sheen of sweat covered her skin. She was pushing every limit just to keep up with this black-clad man, and she wasn't sure why.

Scratch that, she knew exactly why.

Charlissa had mentioned Anya's mother—not as a hypothetical concept, but by name. She used her mother's name. It was a mystery at Anya's core. What had happened to Sofia Corazon? Why had she left her and Papi all those years ago? Could she have been a Hunter, like Miguel or this Wasp lady? Or had something else happened? Anya had to find out—and right now, Miguel was the closest thing she had to an answer.

She saw the trees parting and could hear the soothing sounds of Fort Greene traffic—the honking horns, the profanities of passersby, and the light smell of garbage and cigarette smoke. They were almost there. Almost home free.

A short *slash* sliced through the din of the city. Anya ignored it, but she saw Miguel looking back, concern on his face. Anya was confused—why was he stopping? Then she realized she was stopping, too. The pain came soon after—a deep, throbbing pain emanating from her midsection. She reached out to touch it and was terrified by what she saw and felt.

The pain got worse. The throbbing, dull ache replaced by an anguish she couldn't truly comprehend. Every part of her was in agony. But that wasn't the worst part. No, what would forever haunt Anya was what she saw—blood everywhere, and a long, silver-tipped arrow jutting through her midsection.

"Stay awake."

The words seemed to come into focus slowly, like clouds crashing together. Anya was on the ground, lying on her side. She could see an arrow, coated in blood, a few feet away. *The arrow they shot through me.*

She coughed. She felt something warm and coppery tasting in her mouth. *Blood.* Her own blood, she realized. Miguel was waving his hands over her, mumbling to himself. Anya thought she saw flickers of light shooting from his fingertips, trailing them like some kind of Fourth of July sparkler. But she must have been imagining this, she thought—some kind of side effect from being inches from death.

She felt her eyelids grow heavy, and she longed for

sleep. The pain in her midsection was still there, dull, throbbing, and impossible to ignore. She just wanted to sleep and wake up and feel better.

"Anya, do not go to sleep," Miguel said, interrupting his incantation. "I can't keep you alive—awake, I mean—and finish this."

He locked eyes with her.

"I need something, anything that you have on you, anything of great personal value," he said. His words were quick and frantic. "Think, Anya. Think."

Anya couldn't. She couldn't think, period. But Miguel seemed to sense something, because he watched her intently as her hand reached for the tiny purple amulet that she wore around her neck. She'd clutched it instinctively, like a kid gripping a blanket in the dark. Wearing it was so ingrained in her, she didn't even notice.

"That necklace," Miguel said, his voice almost panicked. "Who gave it to you?"

"My—uh—my mom," Anya said. She could barely get the words out. She was hurting, tired. She felt ready to let go. "Before she . . . guh . . . left."

But she couldn't. She wouldn't.

Miguel yanked the necklace off her, the band snapping. She wanted to get up and take it back—to smack this strange man for taking the one thing she had left of her mother's. But she was so tired.

Miguel started mumbling again, the lights surrounding him growing brighter. She felt the blood draining out of her body. The cold of the New York pavement under her. She shivered. Not a chill, but a bone-shaking spasm. Her body was winding down, she realized. She felt herself floating above the supine form on the edge of Fort Greene Park, and wondered what was going to happen next. Would she see her abuelo? Her mom? Miguel's form started to fade, the light show he was conducting growing bigger and brighter. Eventually, the brightness consumed everything Anya saw, enveloping her. Soon she felt her eyes close.

She was gone.

The dreams came then. Or were they visions? She'd never be sure.

Anya saw herself—as if she were floating above, looking down on herself as she went about her daily routines. Small talk with friends on the bus. Studying with Lynn and their friend Ezra in the library. Texting her papi from the media room to let him know she'd be late—another deadline to meet. He understood, of course. His life was built around deadlines. Anya watched as she changed into workout clothes and went through her usual gymnastics warm-ups, each one growing more difficult than the last. Focused. Always grinding. Even at the stuff she wasn't particularly good at—like gymnastics. Pushed forward by a passion and dedication that felt almost embedded in her. Anya was always moving and on the go. No time for video games, television, distractions. She was focused, and even now—in this detached, strange series of vignettes—she could see herself stretching and straining to do more. From this vantage point, from this bizarre perspective, she gained a grudging admiration for herself. For her work ethic and ability to focus. Anya Corazon didn't sleepwalk through life—she pressed on. But the dream-vision turned dark as she arrived home. As she stumbled into her room and her eyes—her own and the eyes of the Anya she was watching—moved to her nightstand. To an aging photo, framed and propped up next to her bed. Two people cradling a small baby. The smile was unmistakable, even now. It was Anya, flanked by a younger Gilberto and Sofia. But now Sofia's eyes were glowing, black tears trailing down her cheeks. Anya—both Anyas—screamed, the sound cracking the vision in half, the pieces of the dream-world falling into an endless, dark void.

When her eyes fluttered open again, she was in darkness. Not complete, but dark enough that she could only see a tiny sliver of light, as if held up by a tightly wound net. She was also elevated, she realized. But where? She reached for her neck, feeling for the amulet—but it was gone. Then her hand traced the area of her midsection—the place that had been gushing blood, pulsing with pain from a surefire mortal injury. But all that she found was smooth skin. And what was that itchy feeling on her arm? Anya kicked out with her feet—expecting to find herself stuck in whatever trap this was. Instead, her foot went right through—as if she'd been kicking at wet tissue paper. But this was something else. She couldn't mull it over for very long, because her kick had dislodged everything. Next thing Anya knew, she was on the floor. It took her a moment to get her eyes adjusted to the morning light. But she was in her room. She gave herself a quick once-over.

She was still in the clothes she'd worn the night before. She stuck her finger through the hole in her shirt that proved she hadn't imagined the arrow. But what had happened to the hole in *her*?

And what the hell was all over her room?

She looked down at her feet and saw what could only be described as a webbed sack—a tangle of thin strands and threads that had enveloped Anya before she'd awoken a few moments ago. And this . . . this webbing . . . was all over her room.

"Gross," she said.

She was alive. She was thankful for that. But she had a lot of questions. The only place she could think to start was with the guy who'd probably saved her life a few hours before. But how do you track down a cloaked light-show-weaving shadow dude like Miguel?

She shook off a few strands of webbing and started to change into a fresh set of clothes. Wherever Miguel was, Anya needed to find him. People didn't just heal from being shot through by metal arrows. Not overnight. And this webbing thing? It was pretty weird. And disgusting. Definitely disgusting.

Anya felt a smile forming as she thought back to that night and the following morning. How little she'd known then.

She hadn't had to look far to find Miguel. He appeared to her as she entered her local bodega, tapping her shoulder as she waited in line to grab a Coke. He motioned for her to follow him, and she did. Because she knew she had to, somehow.

What she learned on that walk would change her life forever. Again.

"Mysterious much?" she said as they walked down Flushing Avenue, the New York summer in full effect.

Anya felt her shirt sticking to her body, just a few

minutes after leaving the relatively cool store, but Miguel seemed serene and the epitome of chill as they dipped and dodged between people on the crowded street.

Miguel nodded almost imperceptibly before responding.

"I'm sorry you had to witness that, but I guess that's how destiny works."

"Destiny? It was my destiny to get shot by an arrow in some weird LARP game that went too far?" Anya said, disdain coating every word. "Dude, I don't even want to know what happened there. I woke up covered in some kind of disgusting Silly String spray. I must've been high off the fumes because I could've sworn I was in a cocoon that I kicked my way out of. But that's, like, next-level weird."

"They were webs," Miguel said, deadpan, before gently grabbing Anya by the arm and leading her into an empty coffee shop. They sat down near a large window. "Webs that you made to protect yourself."

"That I . . . made? What, like . . . some kind of spider?" Anya said, brow furrowed. "Isn't that job already spoken for?"

Miguel ordered two coffees and waited for the waiter to move along before saying anything else.

"It's . . . complicated," he said. "But I'm part of a group of people that's in an extended conflict with another, evil group."

"The Sisterhood of the Wasp?"

Miguel put a finger in front of his mouth.

"We don't talk about this stuff out loud, or . . . to other people that much," he said. "So, humor me a bit."

Anya sighed.

"All right, man," she said, waving her arm in Miguel's direction. "I'm waiting."

He looked around the table. The tiny coffee shop was empty aside from the waiter who'd taken their order, who was now fidgeting with a massive espresso machine that could've passed for Galactus.

"I'm part of a team of, well, Hunters, called the Spider Society," Miguel said, leaning forward, his voice low. "We're basically at war with the Sisterhood—it's one of those endless-eternal-struggle-type deals."

"Sounds boring."

Miguel scoffed.

"It's not boring," he said defensively. "It's quite important."

Anya didn't respond. Miguel waited a beat before he continued.

"You weren't supposed to be in the park last night," he said. "They tricked you—made you think you saw your mother. It was actually the last thing I wanted."

"Why? What does my mami have to do with your Spider Social Club or whatever?"

"Spider Society."

"Right, well, whatever—is she part of it?"

Miguel didn't respond. He opened his mouth but stopped himself.

"You serious?" Anya said, starting to stand up. "I get shot with an arrow, webbed up by some spider magic, all because this Sisterhood of the Wasp crew wants me and you gone, and you can't even tell me what I have to do with it?"

Anya got to her feet and shrugged.

"I don't need this, okay?" she said. "Life is weird enough."

Miguel grabbed her arm. She spun around. She spun around fast. She'd never moved like that, she realized. It was unsettling.

"Feel that?" he said. "You're different now. We need to talk about that."

Anya slid back into her seat.

"Not before you tell me what Sofia Corazon has to do with any of this."

"All in good time, Anya," he said. "But first, we talk about you. And what happened to you last night."

Miguel kept it simple. He'd been forced to perform a

ritual on Anya—he hadn't expected her to show up, but he also didn't want to have her death on his conscience. The problem is, the ritual he performed wasn't a run-of-the-mill thing. He couldn't do it to just anyone all the time. It was a ritual of power—the kind of mystical event that could only happen if Miguel wanted to pass along part of the Spider Society to Anya. It'd save her life, but she'd never be the same.

"So, what, I have, like, super-powers now?" Anya asked.

"You're a Hunter now, Anya Corazon," Miguel said. "You've got more than powers. You're one of us. And you have to learn what that means."

What it meant became apparent very quickly. They left the coffee shop and headed back to the park, to a secluded section of forest, near the spot where everything had gone down just a few hours before. Anya watched as Miguel paced in front of her, his cloak hiding his features. She felt jumpy, on edge, but she wasn't sure why. How had her life gotten so *weird*?

Miguel swung the staff with a speed Anya had never imagined. She barely dodged his first swing, leaping out of the trajectory seconds before the wooden weapon would've made contact with her legs. She looked down at Miguel.

It took her a moment to process what was happening.

She was looking down at Miguel.

From a tree.

She clutched at the branches of the giant English elm tree—the canopy-like growths surrounding her body, her feet planted firmly on one of the highest. It took all of her willpower to stop herself from screaming.

"It's okay," Miguel said. His voice sounded distant. Because it was okay. He looked small from Anya's perch. "This is going to take some getting used to."

It certainly did. Over time, Anya realized that Miguel's "ritual" had done more than save her life—it had imbued her with abilities beyond those of a normal teen. Anya was strong now—superhumanly strong. She was also fast, agile, and gifted with reflexes beyond human comprehension.

She also learned—when she eventually decided it was safe to come down from that massive tree—that she could cling to walls. Or trees. Or cars.

Eventually, Miguel showed her that she could also make her own webbing—literally from her hands. She'd done it herself that night, when she'd returned to her room—some kind of animalistic instinct, a reflex to protect and heal herself after the trauma she'd experienced.

"This is . . . a lot," she said, placing her hands

on her knees as she looked at the grass near her feet, Miguel standing near her. "What the hell am I now? I didn't ask for this."

Her voice trembled as she spoke. Because it was true. Anya had not asked for any of this. She had enough going on—with her life, school, friends. She had enough trouble juggling all the things she'd committed to, just to have a shot to get a free ride to go to college so she wouldn't have to struggle like her parents. She didn't need *powers* added to that. Power and responsibility, no less.

"No, you didn't—but you're one of us now," Miguel said. "And that comes with great responsibility."

Anya sighed.

"Seriously, dude?" she said. "What, I'm supposed to wear a costume and call myself Araña because my papi calls me that? Fight crime and defend the honor of the Spider Society against threats from this Wasp Sisterhood because it's, like, my destiny? Are you legit?"

"I mean, basically," Miguel said with a shrug, "it's your destiny, Anya."

"I don't think so," Anya said, stepping back. "That might be how your magical spider-cult works, but it's not how things work in the real world I live in. I have a life. I have a family—well, most of one. I have

responsibilities. And in that world, I decide what I do
and why. Just because I have these powers doesn't mean
I have to use them the way you want."

Miguel's eyebrows popped up. He hadn't expected
that response. Dude was probably used to everyone
bowing down and thanking him for everything, Anya
thought. But that wasn't her style.

"But—it's written," Miguel said, his words coming
out stilted, hesitant. Anya had never seen him like this
in the short time she'd known him. "It's meant to be
this way."

"Tough, dude," she said. "You're going to have to
do a lot better than say 'It is your destiny,' like some
kind of fairy tale, to convince me to join you. To make
a major life choice. So get to talking, man—because I
need a little proof of concept before I pull the rug out
from under myself."

"Don't you want to do good?" Miguel asked. "To
help people? You think these powers are just a random
gift—like a lottery you won by chance?"

Anya frowned. Miguel was playing the guilt card.
Somehow he'd realized that kind of thing worked really
well. Especially on someone like Anya, who'd spent
most of her young life weighed down by responsibilities and expectations. *Damn.*

"I always want to do good," Anya said, looking

down at her feet. She wasn't sure how much she could truly trust this man and tell him about what she really felt—but she also knew it was a necessary part of what she was going to say next. "And I want to find the truth, too. I want to find my mom. I can do this—I can be your super-hero Araña person, fight the good fight and all that. But I'm also going to use these powers to get to the truth about my mom. If not today, or tomorrow, then someday. Because that matters to me, and to my papi. You understand, right?"

"Of course," Miguel said with a slight nod. "It's only natural."

She sighed. She could tell by looking at his eyes that Miguel knew he'd convinced her.

"Tell me more," she said.

So, he did. According to what Miguel shared over the next few months, every Hunter was able to pass along their powers once—when the Spider Society decided it was time to expand their ranks. That time had been that night in the park for Miguel—but he hadn't found a suitable candidate. Not until Anya appeared before him. But even then, he hadn't been certain—not until one of the Sisterhood shot an arrow through Anya, hastening his decision. The ritual would not only gift its target with powers, but heal them of any ills and injuries. But only if the ritual could be channeled through something that target held dear, something that had great personal and emotional value.

The amulet Sofia Corazon had gifted her daughter as she left her family had saved Anya's life and also changed it forever.

Anya Corazon, sharp-tongued daughter of Gilberto, and Brooklyn-born high school teenager, was now Araña, member of the Spider Society.

. . . and a super hero, too?

Life was wild.

———

Novelties wear off fast. Anya learned this quickly.

Though the mysterious Miguel proved to be a capable teacher, he was also a major drag. Instead of seeing her friends after school, she'd have to meet Miguel in his warehouse headquarters in Astoria—where they trained for hours with few breaks. Everything in her life before Miguel was secondary now. She'd missed filing deadlines for her *Lancer* stories. Coach Menendez took her aside and gave her a "do you still want to be part of the team?" speech after she'd shown up late to gymnastics practice. Again. Worst of all—her grades were slipping. Struggling for a B on a chemistry test she needed to get an A on. Whiffing the conclusion on an essay about the buildup to the First World War for

European History. The little things were piling up, Anya realized—and it was putting her entire future in peril. For what? she wondered. She wasn't sure yet.

Anya soon discovered that Miguel was right—she'd gained powers beyond her imagination. But that didn't immediately qualify her for the super-hero Olympics. In fact, it probably put her more at risk than an average teen. See, she was on the Sisterhood's radar now. They knew another Hunter had been created, and they were pretty sure they also knew who that person was. So if Anya wanted any kind of chance at survival, she had to listen to Miguel. A lot.

The fun part came first. Miguel was clear that Anya needed to keep her identity secret. It wouldn't help if she had a bunch of super villains who knew who she was, too. So, Anya got to put together a costume—on a budget, of course. She rummaged through her closet, dug through her mami's stuff, which Papi kept in the building basement, and scoured secondhand stores between class and her training sessions with Miguel. The end result—giant yellow goggles, a sturdy red backpack, hiking boots, and a T-shirt with a giant spider-logo—looked pretty amazing, Anya thought. But Miguel was less enthusiastic.

"You're just wearing sneakers and track pants," he said, looking at Anya as she entered the warehouse, proudly showing off her new duds. "And . . . goggles?"

"Yeah, Miggy, this is me. This is Araña!"

Miguel didn't even try to force a smile. He just stared.

Anya looked herself over. She didn't care what this guy thought. She liked the costume. It felt *real*. Lived-in. Useful. What was she going to do with a cape? Or a mask that covered her entire face? A girl needs to see, y'know? And if she was going to be swinging around the city, jumping from building to building like some Spider-Man wannabe, she for sure wanted to be *comfortable*.

Miguel shrugged. They got on with their practice session. Same stuff, different day. The sessions with Miguel were not solely calisthenics or combat training—a lot of what they did was educational, with Miguel pulling back the curtain on the endless struggle between his group, the Spider Society, and their arch-foes, the Sisterhood of the Wasp. Though the battle had raged on for centuries, it was reaching a tipping point. Hunters were no longer able to retain their powers when they brought a new Hunter in the fold, which made these rookie heroes prime targets for the Sisterhood. If they could off the baby Hunters, they'd basically be shaving the numbers of their enemy down. Lately, the Sisterhood had proven pretty successful in this regard, which was part of the reason why Miguel was so focused on making sure Anya could defend herself.

But even if the training was a chore, it all still felt very new—and exciting to Anya. She was different now—stronger, faster, sharper. After a few months of training with Miguel, she also felt ready to face off against anyone. To be the hero she'd always dreamed would protect her neighborhood. Protect kids like her.

Even though her secret weighed on her—she was close to her papi, and she knew he sensed something was off—Anya still reveled in the new gig. Hero. Crimefighter. Guardian. It was cool—but it was not easy.

She dove in, hard. Patrolling the streets of her Brooklyn neighborhood between school, gymnastics practice, and just enough time at home to make sure her dad didn't suspect anything. Sometimes it was minor stuff—saving a cat from a tree, helping an old lady get across the street with loaded grocery bags— other times it was more deadly, like stopping a gang of armed thieves looking to rob their local bank, or throwing down with costumed villains like Slyde or the Shocker. Anya couldn't deny the truth of it—those encounters were terrifying. She was a kid compared to these hardened criminals, men and women with powers that put them above petty thugs and gangsters. The Shocker, as comical as he looked, could literally vibrate

Anya to death if he got off the right shot. She never took these bad guys lightly. Never underestimated the blood lust some of these people in colorful costumes really harbored.

Even with a few successes under her belt, though—a handful of nice TV news stories about the "mysterious Spider-Girl hero," a few funny TikTok clips showing grainy footage, a Facebook group dedicated to figuring out who she was—Anya still felt like she was skating by. Doing just enough right to survive but not enough to thrive. So, while she loved the rush—and the attention, why lie?—she needed more than just powers and an outfit. She needed some mentorship that just wasn't there. And no matter what she did in terms of her hero life, it never stopped eating more and more time, taking more minutes and hours away from her day-to-day as Anya Corazon.

The thrill did a lot for Anya, though—most of all, it helped her ignore the memories that still gnawed at her. Her mother kissing her good-bye. The pain of the arrow slicing through her. It also helped her ignore the fact that the rest of her life—academics, her friends, her relationship with her papi—was crumbling.

But nothing would prepare her for what was to come. Still, it'd been fun while it lasted, she thought. Even if it didn't last all that long.

How foolish she'd been.

Anya shook the memories away, her soft smile fading at the thought of what came after. She took the steps up to her apartment building two at a time, trying to do anything to ignore the sensory overload that was sure to come.

She ran to the elevator, tapping her feet as she waited for the familiar chime.

The brief respite from the usual sprint that was her life was welcome. Even just a moment in her own head was a rarity, Anya felt. She thought she'd been busy before—running from class to class, then activity to activity, scrambling to build a future she could only imagine. But now everything felt unmoored—she wasn't even herself anymore, not with these powers running through her. But would all the heroics and web swinging be worth it if she was losing her grip on the life she wanted for herself?

She made it up to the cramped two-bedroom apartment she shared with her papi and could already hear him bellowing from across the room as she slid the key into the front-door lock.

"Anya? Arañita? That you?"

"It's me, Papi. No te preocupes."

He smiled as Anya entered the small living room. He was seated on the couch, flipping through the pages of another nearly full reporter's notebook. Her dad was an investigative reporter for the *Daily Bugle*, one of the major city papers. He was proud of his work and what it had taken to get there. But Anya also knew he was proud to be something else: her dad. The love and warmth in his eyes was something she only saw when he looked at her. She hated having to lie to him. It ate her up inside. The idea that she was hiding a big part of her life from a man who'd given her every bit of his own life didn't sit well with her. It never would. For now, though, she pushed the thought away.

"How was school, mijita?" Gilberto said. "You know I told you to come straight home, right?"

"Sorry, Papi, I missed the bus," Anya said. It wasn't a lie. She just thoughtfully omitted the part about *intentionally* missing the bus. "You know what a drag it is to walk. Ezra gave me a ride."

Gilberto let out a long sigh. Her papi was a patient man, but Anya knew she'd been testing that patience over the last few months. Even Gilberto was bound to break.

"When are you going to tell me what's going on, mijita?" he said, the soft expression gone, replaced by the steely-eyed look Anya imagined her father gave to a recalcitrant source or problematic editor. "I wasn't born yesterday, you know? You come home late, you're not around—when I see you, you're tired and, most of the time, on the way to your room. When you're here, you're locked up in there like you're serving a prison sentence. Are you upset with me, Arañita? What is it?"

Anya opened her mouth. She wanted nothing more than to tell her papi what was going on. What she was grappling with. She knew he just wanted to be there for her—to help where he could. But there was nothing he could do, and by even telling him the truth, she might put him at actual risk. The decision tore her up inside again, this time more sharply.

Before, she could trick herself into thinking she was skating by—fooling him just enough to not have to worry about little things like the truth. She knew he wasn't an idiot. He was one of the best investigative reporters this city had ever seen. But it'd been easier to pretend.

"It's nothing, Papi," she said, hating every word of the lie. "I'm just tired, okay? School's kicking my butt, I missed the bus, I'm just all over the place. I don't want you to worry, though, okay? It's fine."

"Well, I *am* worried," Gilberto said, standing up. "And I think we need to have a bigger conversation about this. I wish it could be now, but I've gotta head out for a city council meeting."

She swallowed hard. Anya already knew her double

life had an expiration date, but it suddenly felt like it was looming all the closer now. It would only be a matter of time before a teacher reached out to her papi, or he somehow caught wind that she wasn't writing for the paper as much, or wasn't just riding the bench on the girls' basketball team, but wasn't on the team at all. Then his suspicions would go beyond the theoretical, and that'd be bad for Anya.

Her papi walked over to her and pulled her in for a quick, powerful hug.

"You okay on your own tonight?" he asked, breaking the hug and walking toward the door. "There are some TV dinners in the freezer for you. And once I'm done with this story, we're going to talk, you and me, okay, Anya? I'm serious."

"Count on it, Papi," Anya said, waving him off. She walked to the couch and gave him a peck on the cheek before heading toward her room at the far end of the apartment. "As for dinner, well, I'll figure something out."

It was sweet that, years after Sofia Corazon had left her family, her papi still acted like it'd been a brief moment, as if she'd just stepped out to get milk from the corner store. As if she could walk right into the apartment at any minute and everything would be fine.

"You always do, Arañita."

Anya smiled at her father as she closed her bedroom door. If she stayed in the moment, her life could almost resemble what it'd been likes months ago—could seem almost simple. School. Home. Rinse, repeat.

But she knew that was a mirage. Things had gotten very complicated after that night in the park. A different, more dangerous kind of complicated. But her biggest mistake was thinking that would be it—that the rest would be manageable and easier now that she had these powers. How wrong she'd been.

She hadn't been ready. No one had.

Death has a way of just creeping up on you.

CHAPTER 4

She woke up with a start. Her body was coated in sweat. She could feel her heart pounding through her T-shirt. She checked her phone, her breathing short and hurried. It was four in the morning. She was home. She was alive.

Anya Corazon let herself sigh in relief.

She looked at her hands as she replaced the phone on her nightstand. She was shaking. The dream again. But it felt so real this time. So violent and painful.

It *was* painful, Anya thought, because the dream showed her things that had actually happened. Miguel Legar was dead. Every few nights, she relived it in her dreams. But the dreams—these visions—held something more. Held little bits of information that felt as if Anya could reach out and touch them. The dream— the nightmare—felt more real each time it occcurred, with more details and added layers appearing. She felt the cold Brooklyn air hit her face. Heard the sounds of the distant city. Could smell the freshly mown grass. All as she looked across a wide field and saw Miguel's body, facedown in the dirt, a sword jutting out of his back, just like that night, just as it'd really happened. But that was where the dream diverged from what Anya remembered and became something else—an alternate reality almost, as if a curtain were being pulled back to show her something she'd missed the first time. A few feet farther away, another figure—one she didn't know. A man with flowing gray hair, draped in shadows.

Who was this man?

"There is a battle looming, little one," the figure said, his voice like gravel. His eyes cut through the black—shining an odd orange-yellow. "A great test that is much more important than these petty cult battles you involve yourself in. I hope you're ready. Because if you're not . . ."

In the dream, Anya backed up—a gasp caught in her throat, surprised at this new entrance. She looked down at Miguel's dead body, then at the shadow creatures forming next to Miguel's killer. Pale monsters draped in black cloaks, their eyes empty, haunting— dead things shambling around their leader. Who was this monster? How had he gotten into her mind? Each time, the question echoed louder in her head. Only one word rose above the noise of that night.

Traveller.

"I suggest you quit while you're ahead, Anya Corazon."

"I need help," Anya said to herself. The moonlight illuminating her small, cluttered bedroom. Her words seemed to float in front of her.

This man, Traveller, would return. She wouldn't be ready. Not without Miguel. Not without any idea about what to do or how to do it. Despite the stress it added to, well, everything, Anya relished being a hero. Loved the strength it gave her—strength she could share with others. Liked how it allowed her to help others, especially people in need, unable to get help anywhere else. It was important work, and she wanted to keep doing it. But could she really do it well like this, with no road map? No idea of how this all worked? The answer was a resounding no.

She needed a teacher. A mentor. A guide. But what could she do? Put an ad in *Wizard Magazine*? *YOUNG HERO LOOKING FOR EXPERIENCED CRIMEFIGHTING MENTOR.*

There was no shortage of super heroes in New York City—but Anya had no way of contacting them. She'd met Spider-Man once, but how do you weave "Wanna mentor me?" into a brief, passing conversation? Plus, it seemed like he was caught up in some universe-spanning villain battle every other week. Maybe she'd have better luck with some of the other Spider-Heroes she'd seen on TV—like Spider-Woman, Silk, or others. She reworked the headline in her mind: *SPIDER-MENTOR WANTED: YOUNG TEEN WITH SPIDER-POWERS DESPERATE FOR GUIDANCE, GOOD OR BAD.*

She let out a dry laugh.

Anya knew if she didn't get her act together she was as good as dead. Because Traveller would come back. He'd bring even more creepy henchmen, too. What then? Could Anya stand any chance in hell against someone who could kill Miguel without a second thought?

She didn't sleep that night.

The rapping at her door shook her out of her dream-like trance. Anya realized it was morning, though she hadn't slept; her mind had been elsewhere.

She'd lain in bed for a few hours, letting the thoughts run through her brain, bouncing back and forth like pinballs in an endless game. The scenarios played out. None of the results were good. She was living a secret second life—except she had no idea what to do with it anymore.

Maybe Traveller was right. She should quit. Leave

this hero game to the pros, guys like Spider-Man or Captain Marvel. She was just a kid.

But what would that mean? How many lives would be lost because she'd hung up the webs? What kind of potential would be destroyed? Once Anya got these powers, it was on her to use them for good. Otherwise, what was the point?

She felt the tattoo on her arm pulse, as if in response.

"Yeah, quitting's not in the cards," Anya muttered to herself, rubbing her eyes.

More knocking. What time was it? she wondered. The door swung open. Lynn charged in, like a Black Friday shopper bursting through for a deal. Anya could see her papi hovering behind her, a "she forced her way in" look on his face. Anya shrugged as Lynn made a beeline for the bed.

"What the hell, Anya?" Lynn said, her face close. Her eyes were wide with surprise. "We had major plans today!"

"Uh, hi, Lynn, how are you?"

"Don't play that with me, Anya, it's almost noon!"

Anya cleared her throat.

"What are you talking about? What plans?"

Lynn rolled her eyes. Lynn Tachi was not patient.

She was not prone to overthinking. She was also Anya's best, most trusted friend.

Well, she had been. Before all this.

Lynn was also very smart and, like Anya's papi, could tell that her friend was hiding something. She also got a view her papi did not—she saw Anya flaking at school. The missed meetings at the paper, the droopy eyelids in class, the B's and C's that were usually A's. The kind of stuff that Anya could easily hide from Papi was right in front of Lynn's eyes. It had spurred the plans they'd made for today. Or, better said, the plans Lynn had made that Anya absentmindedly agreed to so Lynn would ease off on the questions.

Long story short, Lynn was annoyed.

"I told you about this, like, *forever* ago," Lynn said, shaking her head like a put-upon parent. "What is up with you lately? It's like you've got some secret life going on."

Anya looked at her papi for a second and could see concern flash across his face. It was as if she could read his mind. What had happened to his little, precocious Arañita? Now she was just evasive, tired, and skittish.

Anya wanted to scream what was going on. To reveal herself to the people she trusted most in the world. But she couldn't. Because her story—her truth— was deadly. Anyone who knew her secrets was also at risk. And she'd rather confound her father and friend and keep them alive than confide in them and sentence them to death.

"The pop-up exhibit in Times Square," Lynn said. "Remember? The Cuban artifacts? They're here in the US for the first time, well, ever. I thought you'd dig that. And we haven't had some bestie time in . . . well, I don't know! And that's a major problem."

"Lynn, you know I'm not Cuban, right?" Anya said, smirking. "Dad's Puerto Rican, and Mami's Mexican."

Lynn let out a long, exasperated breath.

"Why do you have to be so basic?" she said. "You don't have to be Cuban to enjoy Cuban *art*. My parents are Japanese. So what? Don't you want to, I dunno, experience something that isn't loud music on the corner of Flushing Avenue? Live a little, Corazon!"

Anya didn't respond. The dream appeared in her head again. Traveller. His cryptic words. She felt haunted by the visions. Were they just that—dreams she could ignore? Or a sign of what was to come?

"You promised."

Lynn's words brought Anya back—and gutted her. Had she promised? She wasn't sure. But she also couldn't remember the name of that actor on that sci-fi show Lynn watched every week, so, yeah. Her short-term memory wasn't extremely reliable at the best of

times, and things had gotten a tad more hectic of late.
But if Lynn said she promised, Anya was sure she had.
Lynn wasn't big on emotional moments, and it was
clear this had meant a lot to her.

"I know, I remember," Anya lied. "I'm just wiped.
Lemme take a quick shower and we can go, okay? I
wasn't gonna flake."

Lynn smiled for a moment before reverting to her
usual sarcastic tone.

"Right, you were just waiting on me to barge into
your room?" she said, sticking out her tongue briefly.
"Got it."

Lynn followed Gilberto out of the room, and Anya
closed the door. She slid down to the floor and clutched
her knees up to her chin.

"Just a dream, kid," she said to herself. "Just a
dream."

———

"This place is packed."

Anya had to yell the words in Lynn's ears as they
wove their way through the shoulder-to-shoulder
crowd. They were in a tiny gallery off Times Square.
By "off," Anya didn't realize the organizers meant seven
or eight blocks away, but that was New York promo, she
thought. Still, the place was loaded with people—press,

art fanatics, some B- and C-list celebs, and a few curious onlookers.

This was not fun, Anya thought. But she looked over at Lynn and saw her friend was mesmerized. She bit her tongue. Lynn deserved this, Anya thought. Hey, Anya deserved it, too—an afternoon in the big city, no stress, no baddies in cloaks with ominous threats, and definitely no blood. Zero blood. That counted for something, right?

The space was deceptively large—though you had to get through a cramped entryway that then spilled out into a larger though not-huge loft-like area. The walls as you walked in were covered with Cuban artwork—from artists like Armando Mariño, Pedro Pablo Oliva, and Roberto Fabelo. Sculptures and set pieces were placed in the main aisle, and Anya winced each time she saw an elbow or arm swing too close. Anya loved art, but she couldn't say she *knew* art. She felt a pang of shame as her eyes glazed over.

"This is so cool," Lynn bellowed at Anya. All Anya could muster in response was an enthusiastic nod that she hoped seemed genuine.

The friends walked past the main hallway just as a speaker crackled to life over their heads—a low, monotone voice let them know the main event was about to start in the showroom. As they entered the large room,

Anya noticed a giant object draped in a dark curtain at
the center of the space—folding chairs set up around
it. She also *felt* something. She touched her arm—the
tattoo pulsing slightly as she got closer. The pulse felt
different—almost like it was trying to pull Anya closer
to whatever was under the giant bedsheets.

"Oh, boy," she muttered to herself.

"Cool, right? I can't believe we got tickets to this,
Anya. It's insane," Lynn said, enthusiastically tugging
on Anya's left arm. "Let's go—let's see if we can snag a
seat."

The lights shut off just as they slid into two seats
right in front of the giant object. Anya could feel Lynn
clutching her arm and discussing what she thought
might be under there—rattling off a number of Cuban
artifacts she knew had never been in the United States.
Then another crackle of static, and the same low-key
announcer spoke, signaling everyone to take their
seats.

"We are extremely excited to bring you, for the
first time ever in the United States, an artifact that
has resided in Cuba for centuries," the voice said without a sign of enthusiasm. "Some have estimated that
El Obelisco is thousands of years old. With great care,
it was transported to New York City for this single
event. Tomorrow, it returns to Cuba. This is truly

a once-in-a-lifetime moment, art lovers. Behold, El Obelisco!"

The lights flicked back on. A chorus of gasps and yelps filled the room. Anya could only open her mouth in surprise.

The black curtains that had been draped around El Obelisco were spread on the floor—but something was missing.

El Obelisco was gone.

CHAPTER 5

don't get why you can't just see him at home," Lynn
protested as Anya walked her to the subway station
that would transport her back to Brooklyn.

Anya felt time slipping away. She had to suit up and
figure out what happened to that old Cuban art thing,
but she also had to get her friend to safety—or at least
out of her hair. Sometimes super-heroing was more
trouble than it was worth.

"It's easier if I call him from the scene. That way I
can give Papi any notes to use in his story," Anya lied.
It was the most plausible excuse she could muster on
a few seconds' notice—that Lynn had to go home and
Anya had to run and call her father, the investigative
reporter, to cover the theft of an ancient Cuban artifact. Lynn was sort of buying it. "But I have to hurry,
okay? I don't want him to get scooped, you know?"

"But he covers the city council, doesn't he?"

Before Anya was supposed to answer, the roar of
a train drowned out whatever she would have said.

Instead, she waved at her friend and gave her the universal hand signal for "I'll call you!" before jetting up the stairs.

Anya darted down a poorly lit alley and yanked out her costume from her backpack. She clumsily put the goggles on first, then immediately stepped into a puddle of something while only wearing a sock. She groaned.

"No phone booths here," she muttered as she slipped the soaked foot into a pair of red sneakers. "Pretty great, this hero life. Lap of luxury, even."

She stuffed her old outfit into her backpack and stepped out into the street. Getting Lynn to the subway had taken ten minutes Anya couldn't spare, and now she had to find her way back to the gallery. She stepped into the street but found herself frozen by what she saw—a large black flatbed truck was barreling down the lane. Anya jumped back, waving her arms in anger at the careless driver. Then she caught a glimpse of what was in the back of the truck.

A giant . . . block? No. It was dark, but Anya could make out some etchings and stonework. Whatever that thing was, it wasn't junk. And whoever was driving that truck was in a major hurry. Anya thought fast—she shot a quick web line from her hands that locked onto the item. She tried to pull, but the truck's momentum was too much. Next thing Anya knew, she was being pulled down a desolate avenue in Manhattan.

But if Anya knew one thing about New York traffic, it was that all things must come to a stop sometime— and the truck did exactly that at the next corner. She pulled herself onto the back of the truck, her face pressed against what she was certain was El Obelisco— thanks to the almost-throbbing sensation coming from her spider tattoo, which seemed to have its own internal warning system that Anya didn't fully understand. But where were they taking El Obelisco? And who were these guys?

Anya risked a glance up and caught sight of two people—a young boy, probably no older than she was, and an older, grizzled man behind the wheel. She ducked down as the driver looked back, making sure their stolen goods hadn't disappeared from them, too.

"You did good, kid," the man said. "But we gotta get paid. Buckle up. Let's head to Bed-Stuy and close this deal, all right?"

Anya let out a long breath as she clung to the moving truck.

Back to Brooklyn.

CHAPTER 6

Anya groaned as the truck lurched down Seventh Avenue and then onto I-478, the entire thing shaking violently as it merged into traffic. Why hadn't she just stopped these guys when she saw the truck moving? she thought. She knew the answer. She wanted to know more. She wanted to know who these guys were and why they needed to steal this ancient Cuban artifact in such a stylish fashion. Aside from the money—she wasn't sure how much an old rock like this would go for on the black market—she was drawing a blank. If Anya had one weakness, it was her curiosity. She wasn't the type to just shrug her shoulders and say, "It is what it is." She always wanted to know *why*.

A short while later, the truck pulled off the Jackie and started to slow down in what appeared to be a desolate warehouse district. It turned into an empty parking lot and stopped in front of an empty loading area. She heard the two passengers step out of the truck and slam the doors behind them.

Showtime.

She jumped off and slid under the truck, clinging to the bottom of the vehicle with her spider-powers. She heard the older driver and his young assistant walk toward the back of the truck.

"They don't expect us to unload this ourselves, right? We're just the drivers here, huh?" the kid asked.

"Don't sweat it, boy. We're gonna get paid and be on our way in no time. Just act cool when you see the people we're dealing with," the older man said. "Don't wet yourself when you catch sight of these creepy-crawler types."

"What do you mean?"

"They're scary, is all. Guys with pale faces looking like some kind of ghosts come to life," the driver said. "Just stand by and be cool, all right?"

Anya felt a chill run through her.

Then she heard footsteps. A lot of them.

"Be quiet and let me do the talking, boy," the older man said as the two of them walked around the truck to meet with the new arrivals. He raised his voice to greet them. "Hey, boys, got what you wanted. Hope it serves."

Anya wasn't inclined to wait anymore.

She slid out from under the truck and vaulted atop it—scanning the dark parking lot. What she saw would haunt her for years to come. The two men—as she guessed, one young, one old—were surrounded by the same dark-robed figures she'd seen in her recurring dreams about the night Miguel died. Skeletal faces, hooded in black, seemingly floating in place. The vision was jarring in her dreams, and even more so now, in stark reality. The faces all turned to face Anya in unison, as if controlled by one mind. It was unsettling, to say the least.

"Maybe I don't get the biz, but—guys, isn't this a weird spot to sell a vehicle? How're you all gonna fit in this tiny truck?" Anya said, shrugging her shoulders in mock confusion. "Especially with this big rock stuck in the back."

"Scriers, attack!"

The voice came from one and from all, creating a frightening, low echo of words as the men called Scriers leapt at Anya. For a brief second, as the creatures pulled and tugged at her, she felt as if she would be consumed, dragged down into the street and dirt and buried by these lifeless drones. But she pushed past that errant thought—and sent a flurry of punches into the darkening mass of bodies trying to overwhelm her. She was free. For a moment, at least.

The punches knocked them back enough to let her leap up and cling to the warehouse wall. She looked down at the Scriers as they tried in vain to climb up and catch her. The two men who had driven the truck over were long gone, probably washing their hands of the whole thing.

Anya jumped back down, methodically taking on each of the Scriers—they weren't particularly strong, she noticed. When she overpowered one, instead of falling to the ground, they disappeared in what seemed like a puff of black smoke. It was unsettling at first, but once Anya got into the swing of things, she was disabling them two or three at a time.

"What is a Scrier, anyway?" she joked as three more popped away. "Figured you guys would be tougher than this."

Then she heard the loud humming sound.

She turned away from the still-large horde of Scriers to see that El Obelisco was no longer in the truck bed. In fact, it was standing upright—across the parking lot. And there was someone standing right in front of it, looking at her.

The momentary distraction would cost Anya, as the Scriers grabbed her arms, trying to pin her to the ground. She couldn't break loose this time—they seemed stronger, more focused, as if gaining power from the obelisk and whoever was controlling them. The tattoo on her arm was throbbing, too, almost in unison with El Obelisco's vibrations.

Anya writhed, trying to loosen the Scriers' grip, but to no avail. The shadowy figure that had stood in front of the artifact was now moving toward her—and she felt a sinking recognition. She also felt a realization— the kind of thought that crosses your mind way too late to make a difference.

She hadn't stumbled upon the drivers because she was a great detective. She hadn't fought off the Scriers because she was a skilled hand-to-hand combatant.

They *wanted* her here.

The shadowy figure stepped into the light and waved his hand. Anya felt the Scriers loosen their grip on her. Then they disappeared. She was alone with the man who had killed her mentor.

Traveller.

"You must've figured it out by now, Anya," he said, his long gray hair flowing around his aged face, framing his sharp blue eyes. "Kudos to you. At least you were able to come to that conclusion on your own. I wanted you here—and I get what I want."

He waved his hand in the air, and Anya watched as El Obelisco roared to life, orange and green and yellow lights emanating from its core. Anya suddenly felt herself ensnared by some unseen force, felt her body being pulled forward, toward this strange man and the giant object. She tried to hold her ground, but it was no use. She was heading into the artifact—and fast.

Traveller was suddenly somewhere else—standing next to El Obelisco as Anya continued her gradual journey to it. Now she was a few feet away. Traveller placed a hand on her shoulder. Anya turned to face him. His eyes were wild. His smile wide and manic. His clothing seemed timeless and ancient all at once—a dark vest covering a long-sleeved tunic, gold necklaces and bracelets adorning almost every part of him. He was a man out of time, but also a man with some dark intent Anya couldn't dare comprehend.

"My name is Judas Traveller, child," he said. "Know my name on this, the last day of your life."

As Traveller finished speaking, the energies pulsating around the obelisk seemed to converge in front of it, forming a blast that enveloped Anya. The pain was unlike anything she'd ever felt. She watched as the energies wove around every part of her body, into her mouth and eyes and ears, consuming her completely. Aside from the humming of the artifact and her own struggles, only one sound cut through—stayed constant as Anya flailed and fought back.

Traveller's laugh. Low, guttural, and menacing. The laugh of someone who'd won.

Anya screamed.

CHAPTER 7

No, wait—this wasn't the plan."

The words hung over Anya as she tried to fight back the beam of energy El Obelisco was channeling her way. But she couldn't see anything—just a bright light, with flickering colors on the fringe. Her body felt tangled and stuck, tighter than any ropes or trap she'd experienced during her short stint as Araña.

"No, no—stop!"

Traveller's words seemed frantic and annoyed, like a customer realizing they'd requested the wrong amount of money from an ATM. But they were gone now—Anya's attention was fully on whatever the blast was doing to her. She felt as if she were between places, as if the very fiber of her body was being pulled apart by forces beyond her control.

"I wanted to destroy her, not—"

The lights stopped flickering—becoming a massive blast of white. Anya felt like her eyes had burned out from the inside.

Everything went black.

Then Anya's eyes opened.

She squinted—the bright sunlight blinding her temporarily.

Had she fallen asleep in the warehouse district? Where was the artifact? Where had Traveller run off to?

Then she looked down.

She was up high. Like, hundreds of stories high— on the edge of what seemed to be a floating billboard. The buildings looked unlike anything she'd ever seen— slicker, smoother, streamlined. She stepped back, gasping. She gave herself a once-over, trying to avoid looking down again. Aside from a few scuff marks and bruises, she seemed to be intact.

Whoosh!

She jumped back as the giant—thing? flying motor- cycle?—zoomed by her, the helmet-wearing rider scowling at her with the entitled indifference only a cop could evoke. She spotted a few more of these flying bikes hovering around. Where was she? And why did everything look like some sci-fi utopian city but a bit grimier? The world seemed to glisten and glow, like some kind of neon world ripped out of Anya's favor- ite science-fiction novels. It all seemed to buzz around her, everything crackling with an energy that felt alien to Anya. Gone were the gritty, grimy surfaces of New York City, replaced by the smooth, metallic, and curved landscape she'd just awoken to. She also realized whatever sign she was leaning on wasn't just your typical New York billboard—it seemed to be moving. She spun around. Her eyes widened. It was in that moment that Anya Corazon, the hero known as Araña, knew she was not only somewhere else but some*when* else.

In glaring, large neon letters a smiling woman tilted her head toward a flashing word balloon that exclaimed:

WELCOME TO NUEVA YORK!
The Brightest City of the Year 2099!

CHAPTER 8

Unregistered person, please identify yourself," the voice said, booming around Anya. "Who are you and what are you doing up here?"

It was one of the flying motorcycle cops—or people. The ride at least *looked* like a motorcycle. Anya wasn't sure. Like everything else in this world, it was cleaner and smoother than the bikes Anya recalled—more of an iPhone than the brick-like machines she knew her papi had used before she was born. The guy also seemed intent on helping Anya—he was doing more than just buzzing by her; he seemed genuinely concerned.

"You need to get down from here, miss, before someone with more of a quota to fill gets here," he said, flipping back his visor to reveal kind, soft features. "The Public Eye isn't here to do much good."

"The Public Eye?" Anya asked, tilting her head. "What?"

The man motioned for Anya to hop aboard his flying bike, and, seeing no better alternative, Anya

did. The airborne vehicle seemed to be run by something electromagnetic, the movements smooth but also
focused, as if on an invisible track. The man tapped a
few buttons on his tiny display and sent them down-
ward. Well, not all the way. He pulled the bike into a
small hangar/parking area that was adjacent to what
looked like some kind of space-age mall—with floating holographic ads, spherical awnings, and people
walking around with their purchases hovering behind
them. Everything was different, Anya realized. Not
just the buildings and vehicles, but the people—they
were dressed in bright neon colors, with wide collars
and oddly shaped sleeves. Everyone looked like they'd
just stepped off a fashion runway revealing what styles
would be hot in the next few years. It was disconcerting
but not totally alien, Anya thought—strange yet familiar at the same time.

"You seem lost, ma'am."

"You got that right," Anya said. "What, uh, what
time is it? Day?"

"Time? Eleven thirty—"

"No, like the year—*when* are we?"

The Public Eye officer tilted his head. If Anya could
see his eyes, she was sure she'd observe concern and
confusion.

"Miss, it's 2105," he said, the words coming out slowly, the way one would talk to a confused elderly person or a toddler. "Are you okay?"

2105. Anya's head spun. Somehow, El Obelisco's blast hadn't killed her, but sent her hurtling into the future. Understanding that fact didn't help her much, Anya realized. But she did think back to another time—just a few months ago, days before Miguel was murdered. She'd run into another hero while finishing up a fight with the super villain known as Gibbon, a man in a literal monkey suit. The battle had proven to be more annoying than she'd anticipated, but Anya had managed to ensnare the baddie in a bit of webbing, allowing her to knock him out with a few punches to his monkey-powered cabeza. But, as she tried to figure out what to do with him—it was her first real super villain, okay?—a shadow fell over her. A lithe figure dropped down to the rooftop and a slightly muffled but very sarcastic voice spoke.

"Gibbon, eh? Only the best for Spider-Girl."

Anya turned to see a shape and costume she knew well—but had never met.

Spider-Man.

"First off, it's Araña," Anya said, refusing to let herself seem starstruck in front of the hero, even though, of course she was. "Second, I thought you'd be taller."

Spider-Man nodded. Game recognizes game.

"Araña, huh? I guess that's better than just being Spider-Teen, or Spider-Lady," he said. "You know there's even a me from the future? Spider-Man from the year 2099? How wild is that?"

Anya started to respond, but Spider-Man waved her off.

"Say no more," he said, raising a hand. "I know you're amazed. But don't you have, like, school or something? Where do you go, Midtown High?"

Anya scoffed.

"You know I can't tell you that," she said. "Plus, Midtown is for bougie Queens kids. Wouldn't be caught dead there."

Spider-Man seemed to stiffen. If Anya knew any better, she'd think she'd offended the guy.

"Well, I can take it from here," he said, motioning toward the tied-up Gibbon. "You can go back to your homework or whatever it is the youths do these days? TikChek or Spacebook."

But it wasn't the jokes that lingered with Anya now, as she watched the future unfurl before her eyes. It was something her Spider-Man had said. 2099 wasn't that far from 2105, which meant there might be a

Spider-Man here. And a Spider-Man meant she might have a chance to get back home. Anya could use all the hope she could muster right about now.

And there was one thing she was sure of: Spider-Man meant hope.

CHAPTER 9

"Dim lights thirty percent."

The expansive executive office, atop the iconic Alchemax building, darkened accordingly. The room was spacious—the size of what many people downtown would kill to live in. It was a mishmash of various workstations, floor-to-ceiling computer screens, and a massive, floating plank of metal that served as a desk. In years past, this space was pristine, organized, with nary a holo-chron out of place. But it wasn't a working space. At least Miguel O'Hara didn't think so.

The CEO of Alchemax sat behind the massive desk, his fingers massaging his temples, his eyes closed. It'd been another long, brutal day—endless holo-meetings, financial overviews, and the inevitable company event to cap it off. Miguel wouldn't mind the drudgery if it felt productive—if it dovetailed with what he wanted Alchemax to be. For decades, under the leadership of CEO Tyler Stone, Alchemax had built itself up to be more powerful than the government itself—with its

own security force, social hierarchy, and global influ-
ence. Everyone used Alchemax products, worked for
Alchemax, or benefited from Alchemax. They sold
everything—from hand cream to instant meals to
virtual personal assistants to security systems. If you
needed it, Alchemax made it. If they didn't, they'd buy
the company that did. It was more than a "megacorp"—
the term bandied about a century or so before. It just
was. It was part of the fabric of society and with that
place came the ability to push and pull society as it saw
fit. Tyler Stone used that power frequently. He abused
it, really. He'd been a tyrant.

Miguel didn't like that.

Miguel O'Hara wanted Alchemax to be more than
a means to an end—more than just a cheap way to get
things and make things. Miguel wanted Alchemax to
help people. If he was being honest, he would say he
wanted Alchemax to save people. To give them the tools
to survive in a world where those with the means were
able to get whatever they wanted with the tap of a button, but those that couldn't reach the button were left
forever on the outside. He wanted Alchemax to be more
than just a faceless corporation. He wanted it to be a
hero. He was still figuring out how to do that. He was
also trying to avoid the reasons *why* he was doing this.

The Alchemax everyone knew was the opposite of

Miguel's ideal. It was a machine, a service that made easy lives easier. Miguel made it a priority to change that, but he also knew that big ships turn slowly, and so on. Especially ones that made money by just existing. But Miguel's message to his employees on his first day as CEO had been clear and idealistic:

"Let's do some good."

That had been a little over a year ago. Some good had been done, he was certain. But there was a lot of work to do. He wanted to push back on the default setting Alchemax had relied on for years—the idea that greed and profit were paramount and humanity was secondary. But Miguel had tapped into a reserve of internal energy that helped him push the giant boulder up the mountain daily—a reserve fueled by a sense of loss and longing that had systematically eliminated everything else from his life. Miguel worked all the time, because all Miguel had left was his job.

By design. It was the only way to keep the people he cared about—the few that were left—alive.

It was easy to get lost in the weeds of something as massive, as intricate as Alchemax. It literally touched every aspect of everyone's life. There was arguably no more powerful position in the world than the one Miguel occupied.

Well, he could think of one more.

Miguel opened his eyes and let them wander over his desk. The small photo-generator on the far end of the workspace—the only personal effect Miguel kept in his office—stopped at a photo that spooked Miguel. It was from a few years before. A lifetime ago, really. He was visiting his mother at her care facility. His fiancée, Dana, was hugging him on one side, and his brother, Gabriel, was standing on his opposite side, a sly smile on his face. His mother, Conchata, was covering her face—she hated having her photo taken.

Now Gabri and their mom were dead. Dana was long gone. None were around, except for him, Miguel realized. He knew this, of course. But sometimes photos had the strangest effect on you—they took you back to a moment where people were ever-present, and the idea that they could be gone felt alien and unreal. But the photo Miguel had seen was real. His mother, his brother, and the woman he'd wanted to marry had died in short succession. Leaving him completely alone. Solitary meals at his desk. Fitful nights spent on his office couch. Darting his eyes away from the concerned looks and expressions of his staff. Refusing to recognize or respond to the growing pile of electronic messages asking some version of the same thing: "Are you okay, Miguel?"

He was not okay. He was completely alone, he

realized. He was the head of the biggest company in the world, had the means to do anything, yet most of his time was spent here, staring at a myriad number of screens and readouts. What had the years of struggle and fighting gotten him? He was just Miguel O'Hara, CEO—with only the memory of a blue-black costume to keep him company. But in the end, it was the costume that had gotten his loved ones killed.

They'd seemed so happy in that photo, Miguel thought. It was taken a few months before the end. Before he'd returned to his present from the past to discover his own brother had taken up a second identity—that of the Goblin, a villain hell-bent on destroying his era's Spider-Man.

Miguel was Spider-Man. That created a big problem when the person your brother wanted to kill was Spider-Man.

He'd gained arachnid powers thanks to an Alchemax experiment aiming to replicate the powers of the Heroic Age's Spider-Man. An experiment that went horribly wrong. He was able to shoot organic webbing from his arms. Had super-strength and -agility. Could even cling to walls with tiny claws that protruded from his fingers and feet. At first, Miguel had used his new abilities and a Día de los Muertos costume to exact revenge on Tyler Stone and Alchemax. But along the way, he'd discovered he was pretty good at the hero game, and he'd chosen the path of a crime fighter. He didn't realize it would end in tragedy. How foolish he'd been. He could see that now.

It wasn't hard to look at the Venn diagram of tragedy—to find out where the deaths of Dana and Gabriel overlapped. They were both tied to Miguel, and specifically Miguel's role as Spider-Man. He would never—could never—put that costume on again.

Hell, Miguel thought, he couldn't even bring himself to interact with anyone that wasn't his holo-assistant on a regular basis. His mother had been gone for years. The more recent loss of the two people closest to him had left him frozen and isolated, only able to help others through the accounts and machinations of the conglomerate he had stumbled into running. That was heroism for him now—moving numbers around and hoping for the best. A long way from punching Venture or battling the Specialist. He just couldn't bring himself to try again. That part of his life was over.

But at what cost?

The words seemed to appear on their own in his mind. What of the lives Spider-Man could save? Could've saved? Were those lost? Miguel didn't want to think about it.

Miguel closed his eyes again. But he couldn't escape the visions. Miguel, the Goblin mask in his hands, his eyes wild and angry, his mouth open mid-scream. Miguel could see Dana, on the floor nearby, life escaping her. But there was something else. A shape. A man. Over Gabri's shoulder, a man cackling with laughter, his long hair billowing in the wind atop Valhalla.

"Who are you?" Miguel whispered to himself.

He wasn't sure why he kept seeing this man—in his dreams, whenever he closed his eyes and thought back to that night above the city. The night he lost two of the people he cared most about. Had the man been there? Miguel wondered.

His mind jumped forward. The darkness of his high-rise apartment. A small fire. Tossing the Spider-Man costume into it and watching the cloth burn. The emptiness and void he felt watching the flames flickering around the suit that had become like a second skin for him.

Spider-Man was gone.

Just like Gabri, Mom, and Dana, Miguel thought. He had to focus on doing some actual good for the world, not traipsing around the city making things harder for him. That hadn't amounted to much, had it?

Spider-Man was dead.

A figure fizzled into existence in front of Miguel's

desk. His eyes opened lazily. It was a holo-assistant, a hologram that discharged routine tasks for you—be they work-related or as mundane as making sure your shower was the right temperature. At least that's normally what a holo-assistant did. But this was Lyla, who bore an uncanny resemblance to the twencen celebrity Marilyn Monroe. She was also the closest thing to a friend Miguel O'Hara had.

He didn't get around much anymore.

"Miguel, I think you need to see this."

CHAPTER 10

A screen appeared behind Lyla, and she guided her finger over a detailed map of the city as Miguel looked on.

"There've been reports of some superhuman activity nearby," she said.

"Lyla, how many times do we have to go over this—"

"Probably a hundred more times, Miguel," she said, looking at the screen. She circled an area on the map, and it zoomed in, the geographic layout now morphing into a live camera view. Miguel could see the hustle and bustle of Nueva York, but not what Lyla was interested in yet.

"Zoom, twenty percent, section 1G," Lyla said. The camera did just that—tightening itself on a single figure. A young woman, probably no older than sixteen, wearing goggles, a red backpack, sneakers, and a shirt with what appeared to be a spider imprinted on it.

"See that?" Lyla said.

"Teenager with questionable fashion sense at the Alchemall," Miguel said. "What of it?"

Lyla frowned.

"Temporal analysis is going bonkers," she said. "This girl is not of this world. Or, better said—not of this time."

Lyla turned to face her boss.

"She's lost, Miguel."

She tapped another button on the screen.

"Now look at this, in case you need something more direct," Lyla said.

Miguel didn't need to squint to see the next image—which was a view of the Nueva York skyline, two skyscrapers bookending the shot. From what Miguel could see, it was some kind of webbing—stretched across the skyline and spelling out a message.

HELP ME SPIDER-MAN

"Oh God," Miguel said.

"That won't grab you?" Lyla said. "It's clear as day, Miguel."

Miguel shrugged. He stood up and walked around his desk. Lyla stepped in front of him.

"I'm not saying you should put on those nice, form-fitting tights . . ." she said. "But you could help her. I mean, who knows more about time travel than you?"

"Lots of people," Miguel said, trying to move around her. She matched him, step for step. "I'm not a time-travel person. I'm not a super hero, either. I'm just a businessman. She'll find her way back, I'm sure."

Lyla tilted her head and looked at Miguel.

"Do you even believe what you're saying?" she asked.

Miguel's shoulders slumped.

"Fine," he said. "Bring her in. But tell those Public Eye goons not to be forceful—we want to help."

Lyla tapped a few keys at a nearby console and then turned to smile at Miguel.

"You got it, boss."

—

Twenty minutes later, Miguel looked up from his datapad. He thought he'd heard a scream down the hall.

"Lyla, did you hear that?" he asked as Lyla fizzled into existence next to him.

"I believe our guest is here."

"Let go of me! Get your freakin' arms off me!"

The words echoed down the long hallway that led to Miguel's office. Before he could stand up and intercede, two frightened Public Eye flyboys were walking in—with a very angry teenage girl stomping her feet in front of them. It was definitely the girl Lyla had shown Miguel earlier, but a bit worse for wear—scuff marks on her jeans, her goggles slanted slightly, and a snarl that could scare Thanatos himself.

"Just for the record, sir, we were only walking her to your—"

"They dragged me here!" the girl yelled, pointing a finger in one of the flyboy's faces. To his credit, the Public Eye member didn't flinch. "I didn't ask to come here."

"I asked for you to come here," Miguel said.

The girl spun around.

"And who the hell are you?"

"Miguel O'Hara. CEO of Alchemax."

"That means nothing to me. You could be making up words, for all I know," the girl said, incredulous. "Alchemax? No way. The Alchemax I know isn't this big a deal."

"You can leave," Miguel said, looking over the girl's head to the flyboys. They seemed relieved as they turned and left. He turned his attention back to his guest. "Who are you? Our scans identify you as Anya—"

The girl hesitated. Then she yanked her goggles off. Her defenses were rattled. She seemed defeated and worn-out. Miguel knew the feeling.

"Anya Corazon," she said. "Not sure how y'all sussed that out, but that's me."

Miguel smirked.

"Spider-Girl?"

"What?" Anya said, brows furrowing. "No, no way. Where'd you get that?"

"Never mind," Miguel said, tapping a few buttons on his desk. "We have some catching up to do, I think."

CHAPTER 11

The girl named Anya Corazon was pacing around Miguel's huge office. He, along with his holo-assistant, Lyla, watched her intently. She flailed her arms around as she spoke.

"I need help, okay? A few hours ago, I was chasing down these thugs who'd stolen some giant Cuban rock, and then it blasted me, and now I'm here, in the future—and I don't know what the heck to do with myself," she said, exasperated. "I need help."

Miguel started to respond, but Anya barreled on—her eyes pleading as she looked at him.

"I need Spider-Man."

Lyla met Miguel's stare. He looked away.

"Spider-Man's out of the picture—been gone for a while. There's no hope there," Miguel said stiffly. "You're out of luck."

Miguel watched as Anya's shoulders slumped, defeat reflected in every movement. Miguel knew he could resolve this—at least for himself—easily. He could walk Anya down to the Temporal Authorities and let them handle it. This was their area of expertise—managing time anomalies and ensuring the sanctity of the timestream. Though he'd hopped back and forth through time more often than he liked to remember, he wasn't an expert, Spider-Man or not.

But he saw something in this girl—a defiance and bravery that reminded him of himself, years ago. Before things went dark. She was confident but also smart enough to know when she needed help. Miguel wanted to do what he could to help her. To a point.

"Not sure I can help, honestly—but think it over?" Miguel said. He waved an arm around his office. "I have some sway here."

"What, you're like a gajillionaire? Great. Future Tony Stark is gonna take me home," Anya said, her words dripping with sarcasm. "Hasn't capitalism died yet?"

"You need me more than I need you, kid," Miguel said, ignoring the jab. "Let's start at the beginning. How did you get here? What's the last thing you remember?"

Miguel could tell this girl was scared. Brave, but frightened. She was doing something he himself had done a lot in his early days as a hero. Using sarcasm and verbal barbs to shield the panic that was boiling over and threatening to consume him.

Anya shared her story—about El Obelisco, the event, how she chased the thieves into Brooklyn, and the final confrontation. Miguel listened intently, but he felt his pulse quicken as she got close to the end, when she described the man who set the obelisk's blast on her.

"Describe him again," Miguel said flatly.

Anya was confused but did as he'd asked anyway.

"Like I said, he was odd—tall, long gray hair and mustache, looked like he stumbled out of a used-costume shop . . . beads and bracelets and all that kind of stuff. Cackling like my abuela used to when the tele-novelas were on. Super creepy."

Miguel stepped around his desk and crouched in front of Anya. She seemed surprised by the move. Lyla looked on with concern.

"What was his name?"

Anya hesitated a moment before saying the words.

"Traveller," she said. "His name was Judas Traveller."

Miguel stood up with a jerk, muttering "Traveller" to himself. He knew Anya was confused. He himself was confused. But this wasn't a coincidence. He had to think.

He walked out of the office, leaving the lost young

girl and his assistant behind. He had to think. He had to get away. He didn't want this now. Ever.

"Uh . . ." Anya said. "What?"

She looked up at Lyla, who was shrugging her holo-shoulders.

"He does that sometimes," she said. "It's part of his charm."

CHAPTER 12

Would you like a drink?" the hologram woman asked, turning to a table that seemed able to generate any kind of food item—she was toggling through a variety of options. Her name was Lyla, Anya knew, but it still felt weird. Everything felt weird.

"Water? Soda pop? Though, I think the version we have in this time is quite tame compared to the poison you swig—"

"My powers stopped working."

Lyla turned around, her head tilted slightly, as if trying to hear Anya better.

"Excuse me?"

"My powers, my spider-powers," Anya said, her hand instinctively traveling to the tattoo on her right arm. A tattoo that was also fading, she noticed. She looked up at Lyla. "When I got here, when I tried to swing through this crazy *Blade Runner* outtake, my powers . . . they . . . turned off? I started falling, thought it was over—but then they came back, just not as strong. I think they're back, sort of. But I can feel it. In myself. Whatever that artifact did, it messed me up."

"I'm sure Miguel can hel—"

"What's rich boy gonna do?" Anya said. "I'm from the past—I'm like a caveperson to you. Unless he can find Spider-Man, I'm stuck here, and there's no way to tell my dad, my friends, my—"

She clenched her teeth, holding back the tears. She was not going to cry in front of this video game, or holo-assistant, or whatever Lyla was. She wasn't going to let this human light show see how she really felt. See how scared she was right now. Anya had never even left the tri-state area, much less traveled through *time*. She had no idea how she was going to get home—or if she even could. Anya was desperate for any kind of security, or reassurance that she was going to be okay. That she'd see her papi again, laugh with Lynn, scramble to get to school on time—anything. But she wasn't going to show that desperation. Not to Lyla or anyone else. She had to be strong and ride this out, she thought.

Anya was also not being fully honest—she didn't tell Lyla everything. Anya had felt her powers flicker out and felt the tattoo on her arm send a jolt through her, like a toaster being tossed into a bathtub full of water—then nothing. She was . . . normal again. Anya wasn't ready for that. She was just getting started. Just getting her super-hero routines down. But now, without Miguel to guide her, and with her only hope being this spoiled, bratty Future Miguel, well, things looked grim. But Anya wasn't going to just accept that this dusty old obelisk was going to take her powers away. Or that she was stuck here. Rolling over and feeling sorry for herself wasn't Anya's way.

"Where did he go?" she asked.

Lyla smiled.

"I shouldn't tell you," Lyla said. "It feels kind of unfair, you know? This all must look like something out of a science-fiction movie. But if there's one good thing about the future, it's that you can find anyone pretty fast."

Then she tapped a few keys at a nearby terminal. In front of Anya, a floor plan of sorts appeared—it seemed to float in front of her, like some holographic, three-dimensional video game. There was a red dot glowing at the far end of what was a schematic for the whole floor.

Anya's and Lyla's eyes met.

"Thanks," Anya said as she spun on her heel and made for the door.

Lyla started whistling to herself. Anya recognized the tune. It was something Papi used to play on the

stereo when she was small. A Duke Ellington song—
"Don't Get Around Much Anymore."

Anya stopped before leaving the room. She turned
to Lyla.

"What are my chances of convincing him to
help me?"

"Slim to none, honestly—but he needs to be chal-
lenged," Lyla said with a shrug. "He's in a bad place.
Angry. Distant. He needs to be reminded that the
world isn't all board meetings and mergers. That
there are people he can help in a different way. He's
become a real sad sack lately. Maybe you can help him
with that?"

Anya nodded and walked out.

"I need your help."

Anya's words echoed through the long, empty conference room. The central table seemed to float in
place, surrounded by chairs that had no legs, with
floating screens hovering around a figure at the far
end. She assumed that was Miguel. She couldn't tell,
because the room was completely shrouded in darkness.

"I'm not a hero."

The voice that spoke the words was hoarse. Anya

thought she caught a glimmer of Miguel's eyes, the light from the hallway creeping into the room.

"How do you turn lights on in this place?" she asked, stepping in. "Clap your hands?"

"Lights," Miguel said.

The room brightened immediately. Anya covered her eyes, squinting from the sudden illumination. Every space, every inch of this world felt new and different to her. It was unnerving, as if she'd walked into a carnival fun house and couldn't find her way back out. She could feel her mind spinning, straining to find something glib or funny to say—anything that could throw a smoke screen around her and prevent people from seeing just how terrified she was.

"Makes sense," Anya said, lowering her arms. She took a seat near Miguel. "So . . . can we talk?"

Miguel leaned back in his chair and looked Anya over. She could sense genuine worry in his eyes—but it was paired with something else. Insecurity. Fear. Hesitation? Lots of sadness, too. Anya's life had not been free of tragedy, but she shuddered to think about what Miguel had experienced.

"There's not much to say. You need a hero, and I'm not it. But sure, shoot," Miguel said. "That's a twencen saying, right?"

"Twencen?"

"Twentieth century," Miguel said. "Or twentieth-century adjacent. Your time period, basically."

Anya shook her head.

"Yeah, sure, I mean—whatever?" Anya said. "I need help. I'm stuck here. I told Lyla this, but whatever blasted me is draining my powers. I don't know how I'm gonna get out of this mess. Is there anyone who can help me? Do you have a lead on the Spider-Man that protects this timeline?"

"I told you, he's gone," Miguel said, his tone terse and immovable. "I can't help you there. Not in the way you need. I can try to talk to some people—Alchemax has a whole team dedicated to exploring time travel—but I don't know if they're able to just . . . send you back."

"I don't want to just go back," Anya said. "I want my powers fixed. They're coming back now, I can feel them—but this situation is not ideal. I want things to go back to how they were. And I want to send a fist through this Traveller dude's smarmy face."

Miguel seemed to freeze at the mention of the name. Anya wasn't sure why, but it worried her nonetheless. His eyes glazed over, brow furrowed, as if he were being transported somewhere else—somewhere bad. This guy was in a seriously bad headspace, Anya thought.

"I can't—I won't help you find Spider-Man. He's gone. He will never come back. You need to get that through your head," Miguel said, his tone harsh and annoyed, as if angrily reading from a script he'd repeated aloud dozens of times already. "I'm not sure what else to say. I'll try to figure out a way to get you back to your time. I—"

"No, you don't get it, Mr. Big-Deal Kajillionaire Corporate Drone—I can't go back. Not like this. My powers are on the fritz, probably disappearing, and I'm not ready for that."

"For what?" Miguel said, turning to look at Anya directly. "I'd be celebrating if I were you."

"What?"

"To have no powers? No responsibilities? To get to be a kid?" Miguel said, eyes widening. "Don't write that off. That chance for normalcy. We don't all get that, okay? What more could you want from life?"

Anya stood up and backed away toward the door she'd entered from.

"What more do I want? I want to do some good. To be a hero. Why can't you understand that?" Anya said, her eyes squinting in confusion and anger. "Not everyone can just sit back and watch people count their money for them. People need help. I want to learn how to help them. Guess you're not the answer. What the hell happened to you?"

Anya backed out of the doorway. She thought she could see Miguel's head hang down as the automatic door hissed shut.

"I'm leaving," Anya announced as she entered Miguel's office. Lyla turned at the noise but didn't seem surprised.

"I guess Miguel didn't give you the hard sell," she said.

"He's useless," Anya said, looking out the large window that took up most of the space behind Miguel's massive desk. "Why would Spider-Man befriend a loser like him?"

Lyla scrunched her nose.

"Well, even if he can't find you Spider-Man—who, to be fair, has been missing for years—Miguel can at least help you, if he gets off his chair," Lyla said, her head tilting slightly, as if in thought. "Alchemax is no slouch. The company is tapped into every part of the world. I mean, surely someone could get you back to your—"

"I don't want to just go back home!" Anya said, slamming a fist into the window glass, a low *thump* emanating from the spot. "Why do people in this shiny, happy future have to be convinced to do the right thing? He's just like any other megacorp CEO—cashing his checks and wasting money on silly things but not helping people. Doing the opposite, even. Just draining society. He just sits up here in his ivory tower, wondering why the world hurt him. He could pull all the strings I need and I'd be home with my powers working by dinner. Instead, I'm sitting here waiting for an appointment with no one. That's what I told your boss. I want my powers. I want to kick that Traveller dude's teeth in. *Then* I'll go home. Why is that so hard to understand?"

"Not hard to understand at all," Lyla said. She'd moved to the far west corner of the office and seemed to be staring at something in the distance. "Um, did that follow you here?"

Anya spun around and tried to see what Lyla was seeing.

"What?"

She moved closer to Lyla and saw what the holo-assistant was talking about. It sent a shock through her.

What appeared to be a giant demon, its long red tongue hanging out of its mouth, was flying toward them on a large, winged glider that also happened to be alive. And on fire. Anya thought she could hear the monster screeching through the layered glass of the office. Worst of all—it was carrying two innocent bystanders.

Anya looked at Lyla; she could see numbers and figures rolling over her eyes.

"What is that?" Lyla asked. "I'm not finding anything in my files. And my files are quite thorough."

"It's some kind of Green Goblin wannabe. There are a lot of those in my time," Anya said, sliding her Araña goggles over her eyes.

"Here, too," Lyla said, shaking her head softly. There's something there, Anya thought. But now wasn't the time to dig deeper.

She looked at Lyla.

"There an easy way out this window, or do I need to hit the button for the lobby?"

"One thing you'll learn here, kid," Lyla said as she tapped a button. A second later, the main windows opened with a *shoom*. "I'm more decisive than my boss."

Anya gave Lyla a thumbs-up as she leapt out. She thought she heard Lyla say something to herself as she swung toward danger:

"I like her."

CHAPTER 13

Another sinner?!"

The scream was otherworldly—primal and monstrous. Anya almost stopped mid-swing. The fear crashed into her like a wave. She already felt out of sorts. She'd half expected to see her version of the New York skyline when she leapt from the Alchemax building. Instead, she'd felt her senses overloaded by the pure architectural wizardry of the year 2105. Buildings were no longer just pillars stacked to the skies—they seemed to come in all shapes and sizes, curving up and out, spheres and ovals instead of blocks and rectangles. The colors, too, were all over the place—glittering neon signs competed with each other, holographic advertisements sped in every direction, orange and green and yellow buildings and cars seemed to compete with each other for real estate in Anya's field of vision. It was as if someone had fed the idea of New York through the filter of Roy Lichtenstein paintings. It was bright, loud, oddly familiar, and impossible to ignore. She felt delirious and confused. How was she going to get out of here? More importantly, why had this modern-day creature decided to show up now? In the *future*?

The monster, known as Demogoblin, was clutching two innocent people, who seemed even more scared than Anya was. The creature—which Anya had only learned about after going down one particularly long "villain research" rabbit hole a few weeks back—was a literal demon that had once been merged with Spidey baddie Hobgoblin, and was dangling both of his victims over his shoulder like one would carry a purse. The casual air added to Anya's panic—this monster wouldn't hesitate for a second if dropping his captives would give him the upper hand in a fight.

"Sinner? You're literally the one with the fangs and scales, bud," Anya said, tugging on her webbing to dodge the first of what would surely be dozens of hellfire-coated pumpkin bombs. "Seems like you're projecting a bit."

The Demogoblin pivoted—swerving his glider around Anya, moving faster than she could see. She tried to turn herself around but felt a familiar dizziness. The tattoo on her arm was throbbing, and for a second, she felt helpless—as if she were dangling from a piece of rope, stories above the ground, with no way of staying up there.

She fell—for a second—but managed to grab her web

and swing herself to a nearby rooftop. She needed a minute to regroup. But she wouldn't get half that. Anya could already see the Demogoblin speeding toward her, the man and woman he'd captured tucked under each arm. They were wearing what Anya assumed was typical garb for the time—bodysuits that seemed more like futuristic onesies than the usual stuff she'd see in Fort Greene. But fashion notwithstanding, Anya had to do something—even if her abilities were as reliable as the G train at rush hour.

Her powers were flickering badly, Anya knew. They could fizzle out at any second. But she had to do something. She had to stop this monster, even if it meant dying here—in the future, away from her family, friends, and home. It's what heroes did, right?

"You will pay, sinner! You will fall victim to my righteous fury!" the demon screeched. The monster was close enough that Anya could see the two prisoners wincing as the sound invaded their ears. "You have brought me to this world, to this haven of the damned—and now my work is never complete!"

Anya's arm jutted out instinctively, as if she was trying to shoot a strand of webbing to get herself out of harm's way. She couldn't do that—her powers had fizzled. But she felt something—a familiar tingling on her arm. The tattoo. Familiar but muted, as if the tattoo was trying to force itself through, past the restraints the artifact had enveloped her in. She didn't know what it meant, but maybe she had some power—some juice left before it was too late.

She felt the webbing shoot out, a short, stunted burst, then felt her arm tingle with pain—as if sharp needles were being shoved into her flesh over and over. She felt herself keel over, her good arm clutching the other, the tattoo thrumming almost violently. She wanted to tear her arm off, but she also wanted to live. She spared a glance up and heard what had happened before she saw it—a frustrated squeal of surprise that seemed to echo throughout the smooth, streamlined buildings of this future utopia. When Anya did manage to look up, she saw that her shot, as shaky as it was, had hit home—landing squarely in the Demogoblin's large, red-tinged eyes.

The monster was flailing now, and Anya leapt to catch the two prisoners as he let them fall. Thankfully, it wasn't a huge drop—the Demogoblin had been closer than Anya wanted to think after all.

"What the shock was that thing?" the woman asked, her voice laced with panic. "It felt so dark . . . so evil."

"Just run, lady," Anya said, stepping in front of the

man and woman, both around her papi's age. "And pray you never see this thing again."

"Works for me, kid," the man said, not hesitating to speed toward the far side of the building roof, presumably to some kind of safety. Anya didn't have time to check.

The Demogoblin had recovered—Anya noticed claw marks around his eyes, and she couldn't shake the smell of burning flesh. *Did he char the webbing off his face?* She didn't want to know. What she did know, though, was that he was riding his living monster glider toward her, and she wasn't sure how much power she had left. It felt like a terrifying repeat of what'd happened moments ago, except she wasn't sure if she could muster another last-minute power boost.

"Your childish antics are the mask of the vile and sin-riddled, girl!" the monster said, circling above her, a vulture looking for scraps. "Your damned trickery but a brief respite. For all who sin must face the wrath of the—"

She couldn't take any more. Couldn't hear this red-and-black-garbed demon go on another second. So, okay, her powers were not all that reliable. Definitely not ideal. But she couldn't be the first hero to face this. Spider-Man probably dealt with it all the time. She had to just push through it, she thought. Push through

the fear—of being trapped in this kaleidoscope version of New York, of tangling with a literal hellspawn,
of everything—and be a hero. Those were the things
she'd learned even before she'd suited up, even before
she'd gotten her powers. She'd seen her dad rush out
to cover a story—not knowing what the evening held
in store for him. Miguel had taught her how to defend
herself. She'd seen the risks they took every time they
swung into the evening. This was part of the game.
Anya had come to terms with it. If she was going to
go out, she'd go out fighting. Saving this future NYC
from having to listen to this demonic blowhard would
be just fine for her.

So, she jumped. She knew she wouldn't stop him.
But she could mess him up, maybe just enough to
slow him down—stop him from doing too much damage. She wasn't sure. She felt her hands burn as they
gripped the demon's flowing cloak, felt fear crackle
through her as she got close to his face, heard his hissing squeal, felt his hot, rotten breath on her face, but
she held on.

"You dare?" the creature growled. Anya could feel
his claws scratching at her arms. She wouldn't be able
to hold on for much longer, she knew. And the drop
down wasn't short. "You dare challenge the one who
shall cleanse this world?"

She saw him raise a fist, knew the punch was coming, but didn't see the rest—she just felt it. A blow to
her head that rattled her teeth and brought instant
dizziness. She tried to hold on, to grab something, to
survive—

Then she was falling. Fast.

CHAPTER 14

She tried to scream—her mouth opened and she knew she was making a sound, but she couldn't hear it. She was falling so fast that everything around her had become a blur of metallic blues, reds, and grays, dirt and dust scratching at her face, her arms flailing out and grasping at last chances that just weren't there. What an obit, she thought. Assuming anyone ever went back to the present and let people know what happened. Wouldn't that create some kind of . . . paradox? Or rift in the space-time continuum? Anya wasn't a science kid. She pictured the story in her mind, in the brief seconds she had left, the sun above her growing distant and small, the sides of her vision becoming darker and narrower. Anya Corazon, the teen super hero known as Araña, died in the not-so-distant future fighting a cheap Green Goblin knockoff, powerless, alone, and—

Thump.

When you're moving in one direction fast enough, no matter for how long, it becomes almost impossible to imagine going any other way—especially when you're heading straight down. But that's exactly what was happening. Anya's entire body was being pushed—no, swept—away. She felt herself being lifted, the speed slowing. She was wrapped up—being held by strong, powerful arms. *Demogoblin?* No, that wasn't possible. She'd be in pain. His touch burned. He'd be attacking her. Someone else. Someone fast and able to move between buildings with ease.

Her eyes fluttered open—it took a second for her vision to adjust, to clear the accumulated debris from such a nightmarish drop. But she still had to blink to make sure what she was seeing was, um, happening.

She recognized him immediately. Not because she'd seen him before—she hadn't. But it didn't matter what century she was in, Anya Corazon could recognize Spider-Man. Even if this guy had inverted the red and blue and was going for a much more metal, death-skull vibe with his outfit.

So much for being missing, or retired, or whatever.

It wasn't her Spider-Man, but it was *a* Spider-Man. That would have to be enough.

"Thanks for the save," Anya said, her voice hoarse, as if she were talking for the first time ever. She was sure Spider-Man could hear the quaking fear in her quip. "But I had it under control."

She thought she heard a scoff emerge from under Spider-Man's mask.

"Looks like something went haywire for you," he said, his voice low and husky. He didn't strike Anya as much of a talker, but she felt a familiar presence—a comforting one.

Anya pushed back a bit, reminded of the monster she'd left flying over the Nueva York skies—they had to stop him, somehow. She felt responsible for that horror-movie reject that had followed her here.

"Wait, we gotta go back—that demon thing," she said.

"Is gone," Spider-Man said as he shot another strand of webbing and brought them both down on a nearby rooftop. "He disappeared—fizzled out—after you started to fall. I'd only just gotten there."

"Gone? What? Did he get zapped back—"

"Don't think so," Spider-Man said, shaking his head slightly. "When you time-travel—well, it's not easy. And you leave a trail. I didn't get a sense of that. It was almost like he was created and then . . . erased?"

Anya nodded. She checked herself for any surprise bruises and only found a couple scratches. Definitely a better outcome than she'd expected five minutes before.

"So, what now, Spider-Man?" she said. "Do you

have, like, a Spider-Cave or a cool hangout? Extra points if you have a time machine and a way to fix my powers."

He shook his head slightly, to himself, Anya thought. He wasn't comfortable, she realized. Maybe what Miguel and Lyla said was true. Spider-Man wasn't a regular super hero anymore.

"What now?" he asked. "We go somewhere and talk. Follow me."

CHAPTER 15

The device . . . blasted you here?"

Future Spider-Man's question was muted by the sounds of Nueva York—so different from yet evocative of the car horns and yelling that accompanied a walk through any street in Fort Greene. But here it seemed more . . . swooshy? The screeches and straining sounds of the past were replaced by blips and hums. The air still felt dirty and heavy, but everything looked and sounded smoother and curated in a way the hodgepodge of New York City never could be. This metropolis was rebuilt and built at once, probably for reasons Anya didn't want to know. Her New York was cobbled-together patches of city, a crazy quilt of neighborhoods and structures that somehow blended together into something alive. Anya preferred that city over this one—which just reminded her of a roided-up Apple store.

Anya pulled back her Araña goggles before she spoke.

"I went to an exhibit with my friend in my

Manhattan. They unveiled this artifact—but when
the curtain rose, it was gone," Anya said, reliving the
events in her head as she spoke. She could still hear
the shocked gasp as the long black cloth hit the ground
in the gallery. "I tracked it down to a warehouse in
Brooklyn, but I think it was a trap."

Spider-Man nodded. Again, not a big talker, Anya
thought.

"So, then it blasted me with something, and that
Traveller guy was just—going nuts. Like he thought the
energy would kill me," she said, choosing her words
carefully, almost as if by changing the story she'd disrupt her own self. "But then I ended up here, with my
powers out of whack and no way back home."

"That creature you fought—did you know it? Was it
an enemy of yours?" Spider-Man asked dryly.

"No, I mean, sort of. I knew of him; it was
Demogoblin, the, like, hellish half of one Spider-Man
villain—the other, one of the original Spider-Man's
rogues, Hobgoblin," Anya said with an "I can't make
this up" shrug. "But they split somehow, and the demon
half is around? Or was? I honestly thought he'd been
destroyed."

"That sounds right, but he's not of this time—like
you," Spider-Man said, pointing at Anya. "But I didn't
see any reports of similar activity around the area after

you first showed up. Meaning, the only time travel, the only temporal issue—like a rift in time—was you. But it didn't make sense. This 'Demogoblin' had to have come here from around your time, but the Alch—but my sources didn't find any evidence of that. So, whoever is pulling the strings here wanted us to think that was Demogoblin from your era, but it wasn't."

"But it also means whoever we're facing can . . . create people, just like that, out of thin air?" Anya said, her voice rising slightly with each word. "That's . . . certainly not ideal."

"Exactly," Spider-Man said. "We're talking reality-altering powers, or some kind of serious smoke and mirrors."

Anya touched her jaw, sore from the Demogoblin's punch—the one that had sent her hurtling toward what seemed certain death.

"Didn't feel like smoke and mirrors, I'll say that much."

Anya repositioned herself slightly on the rooftop ledge, giving herself a chance to look down at the endless space below. She would've been at the bottom by now had this Spider-Man not shown up. She wouldn't forget that.

"Thanks again for the save," Anya said, still looking down. "I'm not sure what's happening to my powers.

To me. They keep fading at the worst possible time, and then they come back, but then they're off. Like now, I know I can use them—but for how long? And will they keep fading? I guess . . . eventually, I'll have nothing. Then what? Does whatever's eating at me stop? Or does it start draining . . . me?"

Spider-Man didn't respond, so Anya pressed on. She had no one else to talk to. Lord knew that Miguel O'Hara wasn't going to help. She could only get so much support from a Marilyn Monroe light show, too. She needed someone to rely on.

"I'm still new to this . . . thing, being a hero, you know? I had a teacher—Miguel—" She thought she saw Spider-Man flinch for a second but ignored it as she continued. "He was part of some kind of Spider Society. Taught me all the basics. Was supposed to train me for this big battle. But then he got killed, by that Traveller guy. I've been flying solo ever since. Just trying to figure out how to survive. How to be a hero and not spill it to my dad, or my friends, to—I dunno—make it work? Without putting them in danger. It's a lot. I'm only in high school."

She felt shame shoot through her as the warm tears streaked down her cheek. Spider-Man looked away.

"I've got no one," she said, biting back the sob and failing. "I'm dying, I'm trapped in this weird future, and I have no one to help me or teach me or just, y'know, be there. It's a mess. I'm a mess."

Anya half expected to feel a hand on her shoulder, or a gentle if a bit awkward pat. She got neither. Instead, she heard rustling. When she opened her eyes and looked at Spider-Man, he was standing up—as if trying to shake off a muscle spasm.

"Well, look, I can try to help you," he said. His words were stilted, his voice seeming out of practice. He looked more uncomfortable than ever now, as he stood over her. "But if you're looking for a guru . . . a mentor . . . I'm not your guy. I'll do what I can to get you back to your time, but I can't promise your powers will still be there. And, look, honestly—why do you even want them? Powers are a curse. A hassle. They only brought me pain and anxiety. Tragedy. Once you've returned to your time, I'm going back out. This is not permanent."

Anya felt her face redden. The tears were now angry ones. Her eyes squinted as she looked at this man, who—different, shiny brand-new costume or not—was an incarnation of one of the bravest heroes in history. Spider-Man was known as a person who helped people in need. Who stepped up to bat when there was trouble. Who went into the battle even when the odds were stacked against him. But this guy? This Spider-Man was just . . . ignoring it. Ignoring what all that stood for. That rankled Anya. Bad.

"What kind of a hero are you?" she said. She didn't yell. She didn't protest. The words came out softly. But she knew they'd landed hard. She watched as Spider-Man stiffened, his entire body bracing for the next blow.

Anya didn't let her gaze linger. She shot another blast of webbing and leapt off the roof. She didn't look back.

"Get over yourself, man. I don't want you as a mentor," she said before switching arms and shooting another strand of webbing. She pulled on the threads gingerly, as if not sure they were really there. "And I certainly don't need your half-baked help, either. Nice to meet you, 'Spider-Man.' Have a nice life, I guess."

CHAPTER 16

Th"hat was dumb, Miguel. Even if you don't want to do more than you have to," Spider-Man muttered to himself as he shot another strand of organic webbing in front of him. He finished swinging and grabbed the ropelike substance and began the movement again. "What the shock were you thinking?"

He knew what he himself had been thinking. He wanted to help. Even after years of "retirement"—or "hiding," as Lyla called it—Miguel still felt the pull. To do good. To put on the familiar costume and use his powers to save lives. Most of the time, his work with Alchemax sated that need. Other times, he was crippled by his own aching loneliness—this sapping depression and endless sense of loss—that seemed to freeze him in place. A dark cloud that prevented him from doing anything beyond the mundane. But this time, the pull to make a difference defeated the fear and anxiety that had clouded him since that dark night.

Since his brother Gabriel's death.

But there was something about this girl—Anya—that

made the pull stronger. He wanted to not only help her but teach her. Pass along some of the knowledge he'd been burying since Gabri's death. Her story, about her own Miguel, resonated. Miguel kind of hated himself for caring. He thought he was past that. Past worrying about other people and trying to help that way. Look how far it had gotten him, he thought.

Tiny claws sprang from Miguel's fingertips as he landed on a nearby building, digging into the smooth structure and holding himself in place as he looked down at the bustling, colorful city, past the flying Public Eye officers, the mag-cars, and the smoke and noise of Nueva York. Toward what lurked below. Downtown.

But if he wanted to help this young woman, why had he brushed her off?

"Miguel O'Hara 101," he said under his breath. "Pushing people away as much as possible since 2072."

His vision blurred as he continued to stare down into the depths of the city—as the other things Anya mentioned to him started to filter through his mind's eye. About the tall, gray-haired man with the piercing eyes. The visual had struck him as familiar, even before Anya said the name, which sent a jolt through Miguel's entire body.

Judas Traveller.

The vision reappeared. The memory. Of his brother, screaming in anguish, wearing the Goblin costume. There was someone else, too—a dark, menacing figure standing over him and laughing with gusto. He was taunting and goading Miguel. The words had haunted him since it happened and probably would for the rest of his life.

"Your life, Miguel O'Hara, is over. Your potential is mine now," Traveller had said. "Spider-Man is dead, and everything you care about has been destroyed. Why even go on?"

Your potential is mine now.

Miguel closed his eyes, felt his brow furrowing and his fists clenching, scraping into the curved building more deeply, his strong hands pulling the metal like sand on the beach. Then he let go and leapt into the space between structures, careening down to the endless bottom.

"Lyla, bring up file 'Traveller, Judas,'" Miguel said. He was seated in a mag-chair, floating in the middle of what once was his living room but had become a sort of war room—tablets strewn everywhere, digi-boards on the wall marked up with incomplete strategies and theories, and food containers Lyla hadn't bothered to discard just yet. He knew why, too. She wanted him to see how he was living, what he was doing to himself, even in his own home. She wanted him to realize how depressed he was. How badly he needed some help.

"Again, Miguel?" Lyla said, coming online a moment after Miguel uttered her name. "I realize I'm not programmed to give you more than a cursory psychological overview, but this is clearly an obsession of some—"

"Just do it," Miguel said, not meeting his assistant's eyes. He couldn't anymore. "I might have missed something."

Two large holo-screens appeared on either side of Miguel, flanking Lyla, who was now leaning forward, trying to get her boss's attention.

"You don't 'miss' stuff, Miguel," she said. "You're literally a genius. You've been over this hundreds of times. Do you know what the definition of insanity is?"

"Lyla, shut down for the night," Miguel said.

She flickered out of existence, her mouth open in mid-protest.

He hated doing that. Despite his actions, Miguel was self-aware. He knew he was isolating in a dangerous way. That the loss of his brother and Dana in short succession had crippled him emotionally. He knew he was shutting people out. The people still left. Dana and Gabe were gone, which made Lyla the closest thing he had to a friend. As much as he appreciated her, he knew she wasn't real. He was, for all intents and purposes, alone. By choice and by his actions.

But that's what he wanted. He couldn't risk pulling anyone else into his orbit. Not now. Not until he figured out the truth. If it even existed.

One of the screens moved in front of Miguel with the wave of his finger. It was a profile of Traveller. The details were scant. Most anything from the so-called Heroic Age had been lost. Very little remained in terms of information on Peter Parker, the original Spider-Man—not to mention his foes, and the other super-powered beings of that era. But from what Miguel had pieced together in his months of painstaking research, Judas Traveller was an immortal of sorts—a powerful mage obsessed with evil and the roots of it, and how the presence of evil destroyed the potential for good. But what would a man like that, a man who corrupted Miguel's own brother into donning the villain identity of the Goblin and then destroying himself, want with an ancient artifact like El Obelisco? And where did Anya Corazon fit in?

Where did Miguel even fit in?

Lyla appeared again, the golden light of her holographic figure shining brightly in the darkened room. So much for shutting down for the night.

"You overrode your programming," Miguel said flatly.

"You let me."

"I did? That sounds silly."

"You like me, Miguel. You agreed to grant me unlimited access to your files. I merely took advantage of said liberties," she said with a slight, knowing smile. "Can you blame me?"

Miguel ran a hand through his brown hair.

"What do you want, Lyla?"

"I can't believe you let her go," Lyla said, shaking her head judgmentally. "She's just a girl."

Miguel shrugged and leaned forward in his chair to grab another info-tablet. This one showed him a three-dimensional display of El Obelisco, with a brief history of the artifact adjacent to the image.

"I'm *not* Spider-Man, all right? I'm done with that," Miguel said, not meeting Lyla's eyes. "I gave it up. I quit. Do you need me to say that out loud?"

He looked up at her. He could see his reflection shimmer across the translucent hologram of El Obelisco. He looked tired and distant.

"And yet, there were reports of Spider-Man saving an awkwardly dressed teenager who looked like she'd jumped out of a mediocre period film," Lyla said, tapping her chin with a finger, as if deep in thought. "Wonder how that happened? Wonder where you managed to find that new, shiny version of your costume?"

"I put that costume on because I had to," Miguel said, his voice hushed, like a pouting child. "I had no choice. It's going away as soon as—"

"You looked nice in those tights again," Lyla said with a wink.

Miguel didn't respond. But he felt the slight smile on his face.

It *had* felt nice to swing through the city again. But that feeling was fleeting. He couldn't do it again—become Spider-Man. Too much had happened. Too much had been destroyed. Too much damage had been wrought.

Plus, he was busy. Actually helping people. He was using his powers—his *real* powers—to do some good in the world. This was real heroism. Using his brain to run the biggest company in the world. Alchemax was slowly shifting from a for-profit monolith into one of the most beneficial organizations for humanity. But it was like swimming through molasses. Miguel had to keep his attention on that, not on putting on a tight costume and punching out problems. If this girl couldn't stay safe on her own—well, he'd warned her. He had a company to run.

He watched Lyla's hand swivel up, creating a holo-display in front of Miguel's face, blocking out what he was studying. It was a full-body display. He recognized who it was immediately—Anya. It was a medical scan, apparently. Miguel could only see an outline of her body, with temperature-guided colors showing different areas affected by . . . something. Something bad. There were life signals and power ratings to the left, too—and they were fluctuating. A lot. Even if he wasn't a biochemist, Miguel could have easily figured out what the images were telling him.

"There's no time to try to just send her home, Miguel," Lyla said, saying the words that had already appeared in his head out loud. "You need to help her, help her figure out what's happening. Because whatever is happening to her is happening very, very fast."

Their eyes met, and Lyla's words seemed to hang between them forever.

"She's dying."

CHAPTER 17

Anya felt like dying.

She'd swung off in a huff, her stomach burning with anger after her brief exchange with this era's Spider-Man. But she'd forgotten why the guy had swept in to save her a few minutes before. Her powers were on the fritz. They'd zonk out, sputter back, then fizzle out.

She remembered fast, though. A few seconds after she'd landed on a nearby building, the smooth sky-blue surface seeming more like a mirage than the concrete towers of her time, she'd felt the familiar dizziness. Next thing she knew, she was falling backward, her hands unable to hold her place on the wall. The fall was shorter, by a bit, but she'd had to navigate her trajectory mid-flight to land in an expansive pile of garbage and debris. As she climbed out of the foul-smelling mountain that had probably saved her life, all Anya could think about was how *dark* this part of the city was. Dark, dirty, and . . . forgotten? Where the Nueva York skyline seemed intentionally beautiful—smooth curves, flowing design, and a rainbow-like palette of colors—this area felt almost like home. But worse. Broken glass. Putrid smells. Screeching and scraping sounds from every direction. It was the underbelly of the shiny, happy topside of the city, and it chilled Anya. Spider-Man had said something about downtown. She hadn't realized it was downtown with a capital "D."

Anya had lived in bad neighborhoods before. She was no stranger to being poor. That's what this area felt like—forgotten, ignored, full of people just scraping by. She wiped off the trash and dirt from her costume and tried to straighten up. She felt a dull ache down her back. The kind of thing her powers would have fixed—she knew she had some kind of accelerated ability to heal, even if it wasn't a discrete power unto itself. When you're a teenager and you can jump and swing around the city like riding a bike, odds were you could probably heal from a scrape a lot faster than your average Joe. But that advantage was gone. And she'd just landed in a huge pile of trash after a ten- or twenty-story fall. She hurt all over.

She looked around. She saw flickering neon lights, people walking briskly toward their homes, their eyes low, an edginess in the air that was very much absent higher up, where Miguel's offices were located. The entire area had a grimy, untended feeling to it. It was also cloaked in what felt like an endless darkness, the long shadows of the tapestry of buildings looming above. Anya felt like she'd fallen through the cracks, like a piece of loose change in a couch or a child's toy buried in the back of a closet. It felt too real to her now. She was lost and alone. Forgotten and unmoored. Even worse, she wasn't sure what to do about it.

"So this is where Alchemax shoves people it doesn't want to help," she said to herself, shaking her head. "Miguel and his pals can fly high, burning money, while the working folk get ignored and stepped on. Big hero, that guy."

As she made her way down the street, sticking to the shadows—since her costume was anything but discreet—Anya felt some of her powers returning. Felt herself getting stronger—her energy levels rising. But how long would it last? she wondered as she darted past an open bodega, avoiding eye contact with the tired-looking owner.

More importantly, how would she get back home? Back to her time? She needed help. It didn't seem like she was going to get it from this era's so-called Spider-Man, either. He was just a blowhard with a superiority complex. Anya thought back to her old teacher, Miguel Legar. The man who'd sacrificed his life so she could live. He would've helped her, she thought. He'd know what to do. But he was gone, murdered by the same man who'd blasted her with the primal energies of that artifact, El Obelisco: Judas Traveller.

Miguel.

Her thoughts drifted to Miguel O'Hara, the megacorp CEO. Why had he bristled at the mere mention of Traveller's name? Maybe *that* Miguel could help Anya find her way home, if she could find her way back to Alchemax headquarters? She knew it was only a handful of blocks away, but her sense of direction was haywire—she had no idea of where things were, and she wasn't exactly dressed to fit in. As weirdly as people seemed to dress in this time, her costume still stuck out. In a world where brightly colored bodysuits, high collars, and puffy shoulders felt like the norm, her homemade super-hero suit wasn't exactly in style. She needed a plan.

But before she could come up with one, she felt a shoulder brush against her. She stepped away instinctively, toward the darkness of a nearby alley, worried she'd been spotted. But she hadn't been. The figure that had jostled her seemed focused on something else. Anya did a double take as she watched the cloaked figure, draped in black, continue to walk down the street. Soon after, another cloaked person joined them. Then another. The line of cloaked people was about seven or eight long, Anya guessed. She took a step toward the winding group. But as she inched forward, trying to get a glimpse of one of their faces, all she could make out was a chalky, ghostlike white pallor to their skin. They looked like skeletons under those dark cloaks, and the visual chilled Anya to her core. She'd seen these men before, or people who looked like them. This was bad. Very bad.

She started to backtrack when she heard one of them whisper to another.

"Do you think he'll be here?" the voice said, sounding like glass being ground to dust. "Judas? Judas Traveller?"

CHAPTER 18

Miguel had never thought he'd come back here.

The idea crossed his mind as the retina scan ended, and he walked onto the lift. Within seconds, he felt the slight tug of air-pressure change that signaled he was going up, passing tens of floors in seconds. Up to a place he'd tried to shut out of his mind.

He could hear Lyla's voice—well, the logic of her words, at least. "Then why have you paid the rent on this place indefinitely, Miguel?" she'd say. "Why keep the inside untouched . . . as if someone were about to come back?"

But he knew no one was coming back.

Gabri was gone.

His brother was dead.

Miguel stepped onto the fifty-eighth floor, his brown loafers noiseless on the soft, carpet-like surface. He made a left and walked to the door at the far end.

Gabri's door.

He placed his palm on the scanner next to where the doorknob would be—if this were another, simpler time, Miguel mused. There was a soft hiss as the door slid open. Miguel coughed slightly as he walked in. The air felt musty and heavy—as if he were walking through a cloud of odorless smoke. It didn't surprise him. No one had entered Gabri's apartment since the blurry days following his death. Miguel felt his stomach turn. It wasn't anything he'd eaten. It was guilt.

Guilt for the brother he'd lost, and his role in that brother's death. He could wallow in this feeling forever. But he hadn't come here for that. He pushed the thought out of his mind and pressed onward.

Well, tried to press onward anyway. The fact was, Miguel couldn't wander this space—this home—without thinking of Gabri. Without thinking of how Gabriel O'Hara died.

It hadn't all happened suddenly. Nothing in life does beyond accidents and chaos. No, this was a slow-burning fire. But by the time Miguel figured it out, things were too far gone. He couldn't save his brother and barely saved himself.

It'd been five years ago. Miguel had returned to his time after a brief jaunt in the past, when he'd helped the original Spider-Man deal with some mind-bending adventure he could barely remember now. But time travel is a weird thing, Miguel knew. It was never perfect, and you rarely came back just where you left off. Miguel ended up back in his era, but a little off. Months had passed. Miguel O'Hara was missing, and Tyler Stone—the then head of Alchemax and the reason Miguel had been cursed with spider-powers—was dead. Though Gabri, and Miguel's fiancée, Dana, were excited to see him back and safe, everything felt . . . off. Gabri had become obsessed with Spider-Man and his own, mysterious return. He spent days holed up in his apartment, taking part in complex, weeks-long virtual-reality simulations of Spider-Man's life and battles. In this artificial world, Gabri was a hero—fighting alongside Spider-Man and taking on villains like Thanatos, the Vulture, Venom, Risk, and Siege.

At the same time, Alchemax was in tatters—reeling from the death of Stone, who'd controlled the megacorp with an iron fist. Miguel found himself unexpectedly thrust into the role of CEO—a job he tried to avoid doing, but soon found he had a knack for. Though he'd always feel like he was most useful in the lab, Miguel discovered he was also well suited for the boardroom. He could look at the big picture and still understand what was happening in the weeds, and his vision for a better, brighter Alchemax seemed to land at the right time. What good was a corporation overflowing with money if everyone was going hungry? Over time, he'd inched Alchemax away from the fascistic vision of

Stone into something almost, well, humanitarian. But there was still a long road ahead. And in those early days, with Miguel starting to get comfortable in the role of CEO, he also found himself starting to grow distant from the one person he'd planned to spend his entire life with.

Dana.

He wasn't sure what happened. Like he'd thought before, the end hadn't come in one seismic moment. Just a collection of little things that, when blended, painted a complicated, unpleasant picture of a relationship running out of steam. Missed dates. Late nights at work. Heated arguments over trivial things. Miguel had steeled himself to propose a trial separation when he found himself pulled toward the island lab of Valhalla—the abandoned home of one of Tyler Stone's greatest failures, and one of Spider-Man's earliest battles.

This time, the culprit was a green-and-purple-clad maniac known as the Goblin. After spending some time in the past, Miguel had come to learn that Goblins—be they Green, Red, Hob, or demonic—tend to haunt Spider-Heroes, and apparently Miguel was no exception to the rule. He'd faced the Goblin before but never in a full-on battle. And this time, he'd commandeered the giant island and somehow rigged its controls to put it on a collision course with Nueva York itself.

The battle had been brutal—vicious in a way Miguel wasn't prepared for. The Goblin was out for blood, and everything he said hinted at a knowledge—an intimacy—that Miguel hadn't been expecting. Who was this person?

It wasn't until the end—with the Goblin bound and defeated—that Miguel learned the truth. He wasn't sure what or who he'd expected to see under the mask when he yanked it off, but it wasn't what he saw. Maybe Tyler Stone? Or another minor player looking to destroy Miguel and his alter ego? But not that. Not his own brother.

It wasn't just the realization that the Goblin was Gabriel O'Hara, but the deeper, darker truth: His own brother hated Spider-Man, and Miguel, with a burning passion.

But even at that point, there had been a glimmer of hope. He could get Gabri help. He could work to save him. Not all hope was lost. Yet.

Then a blast of bright light, and a silhouette appeared across the peak of Valhalla—a tall, menacing figure making his way toward Spider-Man and the unmasked Goblin.

"This is your fault, Miguel O'Hara," the man said,

his voice low and terrifying, otherworldly and alien. "This is your doing."

The man stepped into the light, his long gray hair flowing around him, framing an elegant, regal face that was sharp with anger and disdain. A strange power seemed to emanate from the man, too. So much so that Miguel felt an emotion that had been absent from his heart for so long it took him a minute to recognize what it was.

Miguel was afraid.

Before he could think what to do, the man lifted a hand and sent a blast of energy at Gabri, causing Miguel's brother to spasm in pain before disappearing into nothingness. In less than a second, his brother was dead. Gabri was gone.

"No! Nooo!" Miguel screamed, lunging toward the man, who sidestepped him easily, as a fly would dodge a swatter. It barely registered in his consciousness that he had to move at all. He also seemed energized—as if Miguel's misery, his anguish, was actually helping this stranger in some way. Empowering him.

"Dwell on this, O'Hara, for the truth is set in stone—this is your fault. This is Spider-Man's fault. Your potential is gone now," the man said, now hovering over Miguel, not out of reach but far enough. "Let my words, the words of Judas Traveller, linger with you forever. Spider-Man brought this upon you. Had you never worn that costume or assumed the cursed mantle of Spider-Man, your brother would be alive. Dana would still love you. Whatever hope you could create is now gone."

Dana?

"Good-bye, Miguel," Traveller said. "More importantly, good-bye, Spider-Man."

In a blink, Traveller was gone. Gabri was gone. Within seconds, Miguel's life had changed irrevocably. He had nothing to fight for anymore. He remembered the long seconds he'd spent standing there—at the top of Valhalla, looking out toward Nueva York, the tears streaming down his face. He looked at the blue-black Spider-Man mask in his hand. He must've yanked it off. What was he doing with his life? he wondered. Had what he'd done been worth this?

He decided then that it hadn't. But even that realization came too late.

It was clear, over the ensuing weeks, that Dana blamed him. For Gabri. For the distance between her and Miguel. She didn't know he was Spider-Man, but it didn't matter. He was someone else Dana hated. Less than two months after Gabri turned to dust, Miguel's relationship with Dana did the same—and Miguel found himself in his dark apartment, half of the closets empty, one side of the bed made, and a deep, haunting void threatening to envelop him.

"What happened, Gabri?" he muttered to himself as he walked farther into the dark apartment. The sensors were off, Miguel realized. It was as if even technology had given up on Gabri's home. No one was coming back here, they must've guessed.

Miguel didn't know what he was doing, but whatever it was, he did it methodically. He started in the living room—sifting through Gabri's book files, his military decorations, his various VR devices, and, finally, his holo-library. Nothing stood out. He'd been over this space so many times, Miguel thought. What had he been expecting to find now? Did he really think he'd find some new clue? A twist on what had happened that dark day? Then he'd somehow suit up, battle Traveller, and everything would be fine? No. That wasn't how things worked in the real world. This wasn't a comic book.

Miguel let out a long sigh as he made his way through the apartment one more time, for a final check. He wouldn't return to this place. It was time, he realized. To start letting go. He also felt a nagging sense of alarm in the back of his mind. Guilt over how he'd handled his exchange with Anya. If what Lyla had told him was true, and Anya's powers were not only failing, but she was dying, he needed to try to help her. Even if it all went against his decision to give up super-heroing. This girl was not only young; she was in a different time from her own. Miguel knew how disconcerting that could be.

He'd made his way toward the door when something caught his eye. Something he should've noticed when he entered. It was a long shape, jutting out oddly from the shelf where Gabri kept most of his holo-vids. Miguel reached for it and found something strange and other-worldly. It was bound by what felt like aged leather. Miguel let his fingers trace over the front cover of the dusty, beaten-up book. Of all things, a book, Miguel thought. Gabri wasn't a collector of antiques. What was this doing here? How had he missed it? Miguel wasn't sure he had. But he must've, he thought.

He carried the book toward the doorway, using the lights from the hall to illuminate his discovery. In the coming days, Miguel would regret this moment—and the Pandora's box it opened.

He felt a shiver run through his entire being as his eyes scanned the words imprinted on the cover in blocky gold letters.

THE SUMMONING OF MORLUN
By Judas Traveller

CHAPTER 19

Soon is the time of our rising," the man said, his voice reaching a fever pitch.

Anya recognized him immediately. How could she not? The flowing gray hair. The aged but refined face. He was here. Judas Traveller. Front and center, up on a high dais, preaching to a crowd of pale, cloaked men looking on in rapt attention.

"Soon, soon we will have the power to achieve our ultimate goal. Soon the potential we have collected will be at our disposal, will grant us power over everything," Traveller said, his eyes wild. "Across all of time and space."

Anya scrunched up her nose. So, this was Judas Traveller? The same old dude who she saw stealing a giant artifact from a truck in the wilds of Brooklyn? Now he was some kind of sideshow preacher in the future? The church-like space was dank and dilapidated, like most of downtown—it had seen better days. So what was Judas Traveller doing with his creepazoid contingent? Something didn't add up here, and she didn't like it when things didn't add up. What did Traveller mean by "potential"?

Anya had perched herself at the far end of the building—she'd followed the line of cloaked men, "Scriers" as Traveller called them, inside. They seemed similar to the dudes she'd tangled with before, but somehow more regal and put-together. It looked like a makeshift house of worship. She'd tossed a ratty black blanket over herself to try to resemble the drones that were filtering into the space. She was trying to keep off the radar and not garner too many weird looks, but the strategy didn't seem to be working all that well. She stuck out, and it was only a matter of time before Traveller himself noticed her.

She knew she had to bail. This was not the best covert setup. But he was *here*. Judas Traveller. She had to know what he was up to—and what the heck he was talking about, too. More importantly she needed to see if she could somehow use him as her unlimited Metrocard home. The villain had made it to the future with El Obelisco, and he surely had a plan to get back. Anya wanted in on that. Her fingers drifted to the tattoo on her arm, and she felt a familiar pulse. She realized her powers were coming back, which was opportune, to say the least.

"Don't fail me now, Spider-self," she whispered under her breath. "Things are gonna get interesting."

She let her eyes drift back to the tiny stage—to the curtains behind Traveller. The place was run-down and in poor condition, like everything else in downtown Nueva York. This was the section of the city that was ignored by the Public Eye flyboys and Alchemax. It made sense for Traveller to try to set up shop here, she realized. The future, Anya guessed, was probably more invasive than her own time. Cameras everywhere. Your movements, purchases, and thoughts probably logged and marketed to. But here, you were off the grid, in a way. No one would be looking for him. Heck, no one really knew what he was up to.

Then Anya heard a loud *whoosh* and saw the curtains part behind Traveller. She took in a quick, frightened breath. She hadn't expected to see it again. But there it was, standing tall and towering over the small crowd. El Obelisco—looking a bit worse for wear, battered after what Anya figured had been a few decades of bouncing around New York City. Still, it was in decent shape, all things considered. What was it doing here? And why was it glowing a shade of orange-green she hadn't seen before?

Anya swallowed hard. She couldn't hack this alone. She needed help.

She watched as Traveller spun around on the stage, eyes wide and mouth agape. His arms were spread out, as if he was trying to embrace the massive artifact.

"This is the key to our success, the key that holds all of the potential—potential we can convert into pure power. Power we will need!" Traveller yelled. "And we are almost there, my Scriers. We are almost at the reckoning. Once our device—our amplifier—reaches full power, nothing can stop us. Then we can return to whence we came, and collect even more power . . . more potential . . ."

Anya had heard enough. She felt herself stepping away instinctively. This was bad. She couldn't do much now, either—her powers had returned but were still generally on the fritz, making any offensive risky at best. And this roach-infested blanket was only going to protect her secret for so long. She took another step back but felt that something was off. The thought hit her as her feet flew out from under her. She felt the world downshift into that funky slow motion that happens when you're about to completely eat it.

She felt her body slam back into a shelf, loud clangs and clatters echoing through the building's high ceilings as she slipped and felt her butt hit the ground with a soft *thud*. She tried to recover, to hop to her feet and slide out of the door—but before she could even get back on her feet, everyone was facing her—hundreds of cloaked, ghastly figures, their expressions blank and hollow. She opened her mouth to speak.

"Cool club y'all got here," she croaked.

She could hear Traveller before she could see him.

She heard his footsteps, to be exact. By the time she was able to sit up, she could see the older man walking through a path cleared by his henchmen, parting to welcome him through.

He reached Anya and crouched down, his face inches from hers.

"You survived," he said, a strained smile on his face. His breath was humid and smelled of faded mint. "How strange. I was hoping that drop would've been the end of you. It was challenging to create my own little version of the Demogoblin, but I was in a creative mood, you see. And it would've been worth it, if that had been your end. Then *he* showed up. Which is problematic. I need you both—I need to take what makes you special, understand? Once we handle you, my weapon will be content—El Obelisco will be able to finish the job it started with you in the past. Then we can head back home, to collect the potential of another one of you. A ghost, this time."

Anya was done with this. She was tired. Her powers were flickering off and on like a faulty bulb, and she had zero idea how she was going to get home—to her time, to her papi, to her friends. And this dude was ranting about making things *worse*? About stealing potential? This guy who took her mentor, her powers, her home? She was done with people telling her what to do or what to feel. Did she really have to sit here and listen to this freak-show rant for another minute? No thanks.

Her arm jutted out, the palm of her hand making contact with Traveller's face, signaled by a soft, satisfying *krrrnch*, followed by Traveller's guttural scream of surprise.

CHAPTER 20

The Scriers leapt at Anya without hesitation. Each one released a pained, high-pitched wail—inhuman and chilling. It rose above the low, hum-like sound that Anya hadn't really noticed until now. As if the black-draped figures were hissing and whispering to each other in a language only they understood.

She'd noticed them waiting in the wings as Traveller approached—watching closely as their leader leaned in to taunt the young girl who'd somehow snuck into their gathering place. But now these calm, patient men were something else. Violent, angry, and looking for blood. Anya's blood.

She wasn't having it.

Anya leapt up, sending a kick into the face of the first Scrier to reach her. By the time she'd landed, she pulled her Araña goggles over her face and spun her other leg around to trip the next three attackers. By the time a few more had started to close in, she was on her feet, fists up. The bravado was gone from the

Scriers, she noticed. They were inching toward her now. Hesitant. Angry but vigilant.

She fought back the urge to ask them to "come at me, bro." Instead, she let loose with some webbing—shooting a strand over the shoulders of her attackers, leading some of them to scoff at her miss. They didn't see the webbing go taut. Didn't understand why she was pulling on a thread that seemed to be going nowhere.

They never saw the stocked shelf, loaded with old—stuff? Anya wasn't sure. She saw glassware, tools, and dust-laden candelabras fall forward as the shelf crashed into the crowd of Scriers. Their muffled cries of annoyance and surprise brought a quick smile to her face.

I don't need this Spider-Guy, Anya thought. *I can handle myself just fine.*

She was wrong.

Just as the thought appeared in her mind, she realized the Scriers weren't stopping. There weren't just a few of them—the handful Anya had seen as she came in. There were more. Hundreds more. And they were all running toward her.

She tried to keep up—and held her own for a while—but it was too much. She felt herself get winded, felt her punches miss slightly, saw a kick timed a split second late. After a few minutes, she was out of breath. Blood from a cut on her forehead was trickling down her face. Her jaw felt loose in a very worrisome way. Still, they came. These cloaked men with their pale, skeletal faces and empty eyes. Not saying anything beyond grunts, hisses, and laughs. Anya didn't want to die like this. She'd been thinking that a lot lately, she mused.

She took another punch to the jaw. Felt her head start to spin. Vision doubled briefly. Then another Scrier grabbed her from behind, his arm wrapping around her neck. Anya bent forward and sent him hurtling into another pack, but it only delayed them for a moment. She was having trouble catching her breath.

Then the familiar dizziness. Nausea. *No, not now,* she thought. Not when she needed her powers most. But fate was a fickle thing. She fell to her knees, eyes closed. She muttered a prayer. The same Hail Mary prayers her abuela would recite with her before bed each night when her parents were out.

She felt arms wrap around her shoulders and legs. Felt herself being dragged. She tried to fight, but it was useless. Without her spider-strength and reflexes, she was just regular Anya—a teenage girl with some spunk and style, but not enough to fight off a hundred monster-squad rejects bent on finishing her off.

"I'm sorry, Papi," she muttered, still unable to open her eyes, her head throbbing in pain. "I'm so sorry."

No.

She wasn't going to just give up. She couldn't. As long as she was alive, she could fight. Even powerless, she was still Anya Corazon. She was strong. Her papi hadn't raised a girl who just rolled over. Not now, not ever.

Her eyes fluttered open; she fought back the urge to scream as she saw the ghastly figures lifting her from the ground up onto the stage—right in front of the damn thing that had brought her here: El Obelisco.

"Now, now is the time," Traveller seemed to squeal. He was walking alongside the Scriers as they carried Anya up the steps, his eyes looking more wild and unhinged than usual. "Now we will have that last bit of your potential, my dear. That last drop of your future—with that, I can finally say good-bye. But first, a final moment for you, little Araña. You know what they say about trying and trying again, right?"

But just as she was being brought closer to the artifact, Anya felt herself jostle—the Scriers' grip loosened. She looked down and had to blink a few times to understand what was going on. The Scriers were there—but then they weren't, almost as if they'd flickered out of existence for a second. Their hold on her was no longer secure—but were these ghouls even real? she wondered. It reminded her of Demogoblin, and how Spider-Man had said the evil creature hadn't traveled from Anya's time. Which meant someone had *created* him here.

As she tried to pull away, she looked over at Traveller, who was now staring at El Obelisco with wide, glazed eyes—his expression almost seeming to say that he had been hypnotized by the giant, aging block. He seemed lulled by the glowing stone, so much so that he wasn't paying much attention to Anya or her captors.

Which made Anya wonder again if these thugs were real at all. They certainly felt real—her bruises could attest to that. But were they actual people, or not quite? They seemed to disappear, just like Anya's own powers. Was there a connection there? What was Traveller's role in it?

Every fiber of her being told her to fight, to wrest herself free of these—illusions? No, that wasn't the right word. She felt them. They were gripping her, holding her in place. But they weren't real. Somehow Traveller was creating them with his mind or powers. He'd said as much about the Demogoblin, too. How powerful was this guy? She had to break free, collect her thoughts.

But no. She wouldn't bolt just yet.

As the flickering Scriers brought her a few steps closer to El Obelisco, Anya watched as Traveller raised his arms in the artifact's direction, mumbling incoherently to himself. The device lit up—bright orange-and-green light emanating from its core, pulsing outward. That was Anya's signal. She pulled away from the Scriers—who didn't seem to notice, some fading out completely and others staying static. But she wouldn't have much time, she guessed.

She leapt over Traveller, watching as the older man finally noticed her flying above him, but it was too late. Her feet made contact with El Obelisco—the giant artifact felt heavier than Anya had anticipated, but her momentum had been good, and if she remembered her physics-class lectures properly, her force and mass could move even a huge object like this. Then she felt it lurch backward, a loud creaking sound echoing through the large room as it toppled onto the stage. As Anya landed, she saw a large, deep crack had formed down the middle of the device.

"That can't be good," she said.

Then she heard the scream—low, guttural, pained, and desperate. She looked across the stage to see Traveller folded in on himself, moaning and groaning in a way she found disturbing, as if he were trying to fall into a black hole of his own creation. He hadn't noticed her yet, but it would only be a matter of time.

"No, no, so close," he mumbled to himself. "So

close to the rebirth . . . all that potential . . . wasting away . . ."

Anya scanned the empty pseudo church—the Scriers were all gone, having faded into whatever nether realm they'd come from, if they were real at all. This was her chance.

She gave Traveller one last glance as she darted away. He seemed broken—older and meeker, as if by hurting El Obelisco, Anya had also hurt him as well. But that was something to dwell on later. She needed to regroup now. To think.

Her feet slid on the dirty asphalt as she exited the building, now back in the familiar dirt and grime of downtown. She skittered down an alley, her boots splashing in murky puddles as she tried to make out where she was—or at least how she might get up to Miguel O'Hara and to some kind of help. Her powers were back now, she could feel them—but for how long? And had she just tanked any chance of getting home by putting a mega fender bender on El Obelisco? She had no idea.

She almost slammed into the figure as she turned a corner—the darkness of night masking the person in shadows. Anya took a few steps back, fists raised. She wasn't ready for another fight. She hardly needed one. But she'd claw and bite her way to freedom if she had to.

Then the dizziness hit—the first jolt was light, lasting only a second. But she knew what it meant. Her powers were again fritzing out.

The dark figure stepped forward, cautiously but also unafraid. Anya hoped she could hold on through one more scrap before her powers were gone for good. She wasn't sure she'd be able to. She took a deep breath and started to charge her new opponent.

"Wait, no—"

CHAPTER 21

Anya, slow down. It's me," the figure said, raising their arms in defense. "It's Spider-Man."

She skidded to a stop, a foot away from the hero, whom she could now make out—thanks to a sliver of light from the moon. It *was* Spider-Man. Lot of good that'd do her, she thought.

"Do you even *know* how to super-hero, dude?" Anya said, hoping her bluster would mask the fear still pumping through her from the ordeal with Traveller— and her surprise at Spider-Man's appearance. "I need to keep my identity secret, okay? It's Araña when I'm suited up. Or is that too retro for you? And—wait. How do you even know my name?"

Spider-Man ignored her comment.

"Are you . . . are you okay?"

"First off—since when do you care? Second—do I look okay?" Anya snapped back, her heart still racing. She could feel a sheen of sweat coating her body, could feel the dizziness that accompanied the loss of her powers. She was definitely *not* okay. "I just got jumped by a bunch of black-cloaked gutter ghosts. I'm stuck in the future, my powers are working as well as my papi's record player, and I'm pretty sure you and some mega-corp billionaire are my only friends. Which is really stretching the word, to be honest! So, no, I am very much not okay."

She saw Spider-Man's hand move quickly—it reached for his face. At first Anya thought he was going to sigh, or complain, or do something equally annoying like before. But no. He seemed to be grabbing his face—his mask. Next thing she knew, he'd yanked it off, and she was staring at Miguel O'Hara's face—the same face of that "megacorp billionaire" she'd just been ripping on. Life was wild, y'all.

"Looks like you only have one friend," Miguel said, a slight smile on his face.

Anya felt her brow furrow. The surprise had faded. But she was still annoyed. At him. At the world. At herself.

"So, what . . . ? This is some kind of thrill ride for you?" Anya said. "The original Spider-Man from this era is gone, so rich-boy Miguel O'Hara gets some custom-made tights to impress the ladies? Gimme a break, dude."

Miguel stepped forward, shaking his head slightly.

"No, no—it's not like that at all. I . . . I am Spider-Man. Have always been, at least in this time," he said.

"Bull. What, you just stopped being Spider-Man for *years*? Who does that?" she asked, interrupting him. "What kind of a hero are you?"

Miguel winced at the comment. Mostly because she was right. But hadn't he earned some points for the years he'd spent fighting the good fight? Was every super hero just destined to die and disappear? He didn't think so.

He started talking—haltingly at first, then with more confidence. About a younger Miguel O'Hara, one who worked at Alchemax and was dating a woman named Dana. How he'd stumbled upon another employee's experiments. About how Tyler Stone hooked him on a drug to keep him in Alchemax's orbit, then the experiment and accident that cured him—but also saddled him with amazing powers. He told Anya about the Día de los Muertos costume, and how he put it on. What had started as a lark became a second career as Spider-Man—a series of adventures and battles that consumed Miguel, and seemed to destroy everyone around him.

When he got to Gabri—and to Traveller—he stopped. He couldn't talk anymore. Could feel the tears forming in his eyes, the words choked back.

"Wait, so you know this Traveller dude?" Anya

asked, surprised. Her voice was softer now, as if listening to Miguel's story reminded her that he was a person, too. Flawed and fragile. "I guess that tracks."

"Yes, I know him," Miguel said, slowly, treading carefully over the memory. "He was there. When I battled the Goblin—my brother—on Valhalla. He was pulling the strings."

Miguel looked away. Down at his hands. At the black mask he still held. He put it back on. He needed to hide. The costume had provided him with a safe haven before. It would again.

"I think that's when he got here, to my time—but he'd been manipulating things, manipulating Gabri and others, from afar," Miguel said. "There's something about Valhalla that helped him channel his powers. I think he's been back a few times since then. He seems to benefit from me being off the board—I realize that now. And he seems to want you gone, too."

Anya straightened up.

"He kept babbling about . . . potential, and taking potential," she said, not looking at Miguel but pacing around him. "Like the device, El Obelisco, somehow takes that from us. But what could that mean?"

"Our potential as heroes?" Miguel asked. "Yes . . .

that follows from what he said to me. That he wanted to use that potential for something. But what?"

"I wish I knew, dude. Maybe that's why this thing messed up my powers? Why I get seasick every time I try to use them for more than a few minutes?" Anya asked. "Maybe it affects people differently?"

"I think so," Miguel said. "He's a time traveler, no pun intended. So, he must know what might happen if we're not . . . suited up. Or being heroic. It helps him. Us being off the board—the lives we would have saved . . . our potential to do good? So maybe murdering us is a last resort. Why kill when you can destroy, huh?"

Anya stepped back slightly, as if burned by Miguel's dark joke.

"Can I ask you a question?" Miguel said. "When your mentor was murdered—why didn't you reach out to someone else? Your era's Spider-Man, or Spider-Woman? I mean, I've been to your era a few times. Spider-Heroes are not in short supply."

Anya thought for a second. It was a good question. But she had no real answer, beyond a deep shame that seemed to prevent her from doing what Miguel outlined. A force that seemed to cloud her mind—which she'd just chalked up to . . . being herself.

"I just felt like I was gonna be a bother? Does that make sense? I didn't feel ready? Or like I was worth Spider-Man's time?" she said. "It just seemed to be easier to struggle through it myself—even though I missed Miguel's advice. Felt like I was flying pretty blind, too."

"Don't you see?" Miguel said. "That's why he killed *your* Miguel. Your mentor. To derail you. To eliminate your potential as a hero. To stop you from becoming the hero you're destined to be. This device might just be feeding off that—the losses that come with us not doing what we're meant to do."

Miguel looked down at his hands. At the new version of his costume he'd only started to wear now that Anya was in his time. Had her presence spurred him to do this in more ways than he'd realized?

Anya nodded. She could feel Miguel was right. But the idea terrified her.

"Then why did you stop?" she asked with a shrug. "If this creep manipulated you and your brother, led him to his death—why did you just sit back until now?"

Miguel paused for a few moments before speaking. He sounded ashamed—like a man confessing a deep dark secret.

"I was broken," he said. "Traveller destroyed everything around me. My brother was dead. My partner was gone. I had nothing, and it all . . . it all felt like my fault."

He hung his head. Anya could see his eyes tightening shut. A last-ditch effort to stop the tears. She'd been there. Too often lately. She took a step in his direction.

"It's not your fault, okay?" she said. "You have to know that."

"It all makes more sense now. Traveller is bent on creating a timeline without us in it, and he's manipulating our lives to do it. He's taking the potential—the good we would've done—and channeling it in order to do something else. Something that's probably not great," Miguel said, hand on his chin, pensive. "Is there anything else? Anyone else important that you lost?"

Where to begin? Anya thought.

"I mean, Miguel—my Miguel's—whole world was wrecked," she said. "He died, and then his entire organization disappeared. The Spider Society—they just got eliminated somehow."

"Spider Society?" Miguel asked.

"Yeah, some kind of group that's in eternal battle with something called the Sisterhood of the Wasp," Anya said with a shrug. "But I mean, I could understand why the Society went quiet after Miguel died—he was their leader. It all revolved around him. But why did the Sisterhood go quiet? Just when they'd won big?"

"Maybe because they got what they wanted?" Miguel asked.

Their eyes met.

"You think the Sisterhood is somehow tied into this?"

Miguel shrugged.

"I dunno," he said. "But it feels too tidy. You're pulled into this centuries-old battle, get your powers, then your mentor is murdered by his arch-foe, then . . . nothing?"

Miguel started to pace around.

"Who else?"

"Who else what?" she asked.

"Have you lost," he said solemnly.

Anya's mind immediately shifted back. To her youth. To the soft, beautiful face of her mother. Then the aching emptiness of her absence.

"My . . . yeah, my mami," Anya said, looking at Miguel, her eyes wide. "She left. She disappeared when I was little. It was so random. So bizarre. My papi—it shook him so hard. He just didn't understand."

"That's something, I think. I did some research—I found a book in my brother's apartment, written by

Traveller," Miguel said. He explained the tome and what was in it briefly. "It seems that by removing us from active status, it somehow increases the powers of that giant device, the lost potential feeds it—and that'll make it easier for Traveller to do what he wants to do. And I think I know what that might be."

Anya smiled.

"Guess we'd better show him what it means to be a Spider, huh?"

CHAPTER 22

What the hell is a . . . Morlun?"

Anya's words echoed through the large, mostly empty Alchemax conference room. The only sounds were the soft hum of power as different images appeared on holo-screens on the wall, and the tickers of information that ran over the large windows looking out onto the city. She was in time-appropriate civilian garb, a formfitting blue suit that reminded her of exercise wear in her time, thanks to Lyla's help, and Miguel was in his CEO costume, sans webs and skulls. After their confab downtown, Miguel decided it was best to decamp to the megacorp headquarters and try to figure out just what the path to victory was when it came to stopping Judas Traveller. But that idea went out the window once Miguel revealed just *what* Traveller was trying to do.

"Morlun is . . . well, I guess the best word is a vampire," Miguel said, pacing around. He waved his hand around the large table, and a tall hologram appeared— of a menacing, pale, muscular creature that just might frighten Dracula out of his jammies. Anya tried not to inhale too fast. "From what I could gather, Traveller at one point decided that reviving Morlun would ensure his own immortality."

Miguel waved his hand again, and a hologram of Traveller appeared, replacing Morlun. Seeing the older, gray-haired baddie sent a chill through Anya.

"There's more to Traveller than I first thought," Miguel continued. "From the old books I had access to, I found that there were hints that Traveller was immortal, but that didn't jibe. From what you told me and what I experienced, it felt like it was the work of one man of one era, not necessarily his future, older self."

He paused for a second.

"Stop me if I'm going too fast," he said, a sheepish smile on his face. "I do that a lot."

"Time travel gives me a headache," Anya said, plopping down into a chair next to Miguel. "But I'm keeping up so far."

Miguel nodded.

"So, yeah, he's not immortal—he's a mutant, born with the ability to alter perceptions," Miguel said. "Which explains stuff like Demogoblin showing up— he just created that, or made you and me think we saw that. It wasn't the real Demogoblin from your time."

"I guess that explains the Scriers, too?" Anya said,

squinting slightly. "When his attention shifted to El Obelisco, they seemed to flicker out of existence. But they were also just marching along when I saw them—was he trying to lure me into that church?"

Miguel frowned.

"Maybe. Some mutants are so powerful that their powers are just . . . on. They can't shut off. My guess is he created this perception, or this alternate reality where the Scriers exist, and almost gave them life," Miguel said. "Which, in layman's terms, means they move and do stuff without him consciously knowing. They're not alive, per se, but they can still pack a punch. He's also given them enough individuality that he can turn away for a minute and not lose the thread of any conversation he has with any of them. They only fade out when he's completely distracted."

Now it was Anya's turn to look unhappy. She rapped her fingers on the long, floating glass table.

"But why? Traveller is super powerful. What does he want? What can this Morlun guy do for him?"

Miguel tapped a few buttons on a light-based display that formed near him. A moment later, a long linear image appeared—years tagged along the graphic, and some small moving images signaled major moments. A timeline, Anya figured.

"Whether he's a fraud or not, Traveller is still a

student—and his subject of choice is evil," Miguel said, scrolling along the timeline. Anya could see images and names pop up—her era's Spider-Man, Ghost-Spider, someone called Kaine, and Silk. "Draining the powers or absorbing the potential from retired or displaced Spider-Heroes is helping him in some way, helping him get closer to unraveling what he must see as the ultimate evil."

"So, he's doing this for a study session? To, like, cram for a test on evil?" Anya said, leaning over to look at Miguel's chart. "Evil nerds are the worst."

Miguel smiled slightly. Anya counted it as a win.

"Not quite, but close—I tracked your signature, basically the temporal disruption that hit when you arrived here," Miguel said, his finger hovering over the current year. "And it repeated nearby, right around the same time. That makes me think that Traveller didn't just wait decades to intercept you. He sent you and brought himself to my time."

Miguel swatted the hologram away and stood up. He paced around the long table, arms folded. Anya watched. His expression was driven and focused. She could almost see the calculations forming in her brain, the formulas and algorithms bouncing around his genius-level mind. *Must be nice,* she thought.

"My guess is he didn't expect El Obelisco to just . . .

shunt you here," Miguel said. "Maybe he's not fully aware of its secrets. Maybe it wasn't meant to be this kind of vampiric tool he uses to awaken Morlun. That's good for us. But for whatever reason, it decided not to kill you or completely drain your potential, instead sending you here—close to me."

"Two birds with one stone."

Miguel spun around.

"What?"

"Two birds with one stone," Anya said. "Traveller was already messin' with you—your brother, your ex, your life. You were already off the board. Maybe he came along to finish us both off."

The grim logic of Anya's words hung between the two heroes.

"There's something else," Miguel said, pulling up another chart—a large map of what Anya assumed was Nueva York. "I tracked Traveller's movements—the times he came to the city. When he came *to* your future, he could show up anywhere. But when he wanted to go back—to your time, or the past, he had to do it from one place and only one place."

"Where?" Anya asked. "And why does it matter?"

"It matters because I think he's done here," Miguel said. "He's stranded you here, as far as he can tell. I'm retired. He needs more heroic potential for his power converter, basically, to get what he wants. And it's obvious to anyone that there aren't a ton of Spider-Heroes here."

"But in my time . . . they're all over," Anya said with a nod.

"Exactly," Miguel said, giving Anya a quick thumbs-up. "But who is he after?"

"He mentioned a . . . a ghost of some kind," Anya said. "Can we catch him before he hops back? Where is he going?"

Miguel pulled up another image. This one was familiar to him but new to Anya. The image was of a massive structure, floating just outside the Nueva York City limits. Miguel had hoped he'd never have to return to this place. But something told him he and Anya didn't have a choice.

"We're headed to Valhalla."

CHAPTER 23

W hat is it about this place?"
Anya's question seemed to hover above them
as they reached the top of the abandoned, floating city.

They'd suited up quickly, Miguel explaining what
Valhalla was as they leapt from an open window—
swinging into the brisk dusk. Anya had stayed close
by—"just in case," Miguel had said, not allowing
another word to escape his mouth. But she knew the
rest. In case her powers failed. In case she fell. In case.

Valhalla was huge—a massive, smooth tower atop a
floating base, like a starship docking in the waters that
surrounded Nueva York. The structure was huge, a
broken-down, aging tower that evoked classic, ancient
styles and the modern aesthetic that pervaded all of
Nueva York. It was a potent blend of old and new,
haunted and broken, like something pulled out of
time. But it was also disconcerting. Shrouded in darkness, lights flickering on and off intermittently, a fog

surrounding the entire structure. If Anya believed in such things, she would've said the place was haunted.

"What is it about this place? Scientifically speaking, nothing," Miguel said as they paced around the top of the main tower. "But it seems to have some power over Traveller. And from what I could tell, it amplifies him—allowing him to jump back with more . . . precision?"

Miguel froze for a moment. His eyes scanned over a familiar stretch of concrete—the generic, smooth exterior of this faux city now becoming oddly familiar, the memory stabbing at him. Anya could hear his sharp intake of breath, even under his mask, a few feet away.

She stepped toward him and placed a hand on his arm. He jerked back at first, turning to see who had touched him. Realizing it was her, he calmed down. Their eyes met—through the goggles and black-and-red masks.

"You're okay," she said.

"What?"

"I guess . . . I guess I understand," Anya said. "That this is hard—being back here. But you're gonna be okay. You're a hero. You're freakin' Spider-Man."

Miguel nodded, to himself as much as to Anya.

"You're gonna be okay, too," he said. Anya could hear his voice catch, even under the full face mask. "We're gonna get you home. We're gonna fix your powers. We're not going to let this giant spider-potential-draining weapon ruin us all."

"Is that so?"

Miguel and Anya spun around. There he was, as expected, his long gray hair flowing around his aging face. He looked stronger to Anya, less frail than when they'd last tangled. But that wouldn't matter. They were going to stop him, she thought. They'd intercepted his attempt to jump back in time—but was that enough?

Traveller stepped toward them, almost demure—as if he'd gotten the drop on them. The smile on his face wasn't the usual, whacked-out baddie look Anya had become used to. Judas Traveller now had a different look. Something unsettling and disturbing. He wasn't bracing for anything. He wasn't in the least bit concerned, either. Like a poker player with a full house and a stack of chips in front of him.

Judas Traveller didn't seem intimidated or anxious. He seemed ready and willing.

He seemed . . . *confident?*

CHAPTER 24

The scream came out of nowhere.

A primal, animalistic sound, like something out of a movie. Anya felt her body tense up as she watched Judas Traveller—this older man, who looked regal and refined—lose total control, his arms akimbo and his face no longer calm, no longer resolute, but now enraged and defiant.

"You've meddled enough, both of you, disturbing my precise plans," Traveller shrieked, his arms raised high above his head. If Anya didn't know better, she would've guessed the skies were darkening. But that wasn't possible, was it? "You have no means with which to stop me, your potential has already been erased."

Miguel, brave Miguel, stepped in front of Anya.

For a second, Anya thought the battle was manageable—two heroes, teaming up, like heroes do. To take down one megalomaniacal baddie bent on warping the timestream. But if she'd learned one thing in her short time as a super hero, it was that things were never quite that easy.

That's when all hell broke loose.

"This isn't real, this isn't real," Anya said to herself as she saw the shapes morphing and forming around her. People. Creatures. Some familiar. Most not. All angry.

And, the truth was, no matter how "not real" Judas Traveller's powers were—they were still strong and potent sensory assaults that seeped into your perception. While in the back of your mind you might know that this giant, terrifying creature that looked like the Hulk but on overdrive wasn't "real," it still felt real. Smelled real. Sounded real.

"Uh, what is going on?" Anya said as she and Miguel watched the crowd coalesce in front of them. "Who are all these people?"

"My rogues' gallery, of sorts," Miguel said. "Vulture and Hulk from this era. Carnage and Vermin, from your time. A female Doctor Octopus? The Goblin . . . and . . ."

"The Wasp Society," Anya said, bracing for the battle. Real or not, she was sure the punches would hurt. "About a dozen of them."

Anya did notice something was not right. She'd been in scrums before—all-out battles that involved a rainbow assortment of good and bad guys tussling. But the rhythm here was off, like a juggler with one too many balls to keep track of. Some of the villains inched forward, but the rest—the symbiotic serial killer Carnage, the future Hulk—seemed stuck in neutral, as if Traveller's mind couldn't really handle managing them all at once. This could work to their advantage.

Before she could think about it too much, though, she heard a glass-shattering shriek. Anya watched as a hunched-over rat-looking dude leapt into the air, mouth open and revealing a set of jagged teeth that would make a feral cat jealous. The creature—Vermin—landed a few feet in front of Miguel, seconds before making a second jump right on him. Miguel side-stepped as best he could, but the creature's reflexes were nothing to scoff at. Within a moment, he was clawing at Miguel's costume, blood on his long, dirty fingernails. Anya could hear Miguel crying out in surprise. He was rusty.

The other villains—Traveller creations or not—seemed to hesitate, as if not believing that winning the battle could be this easy. Could Spider-Man just topple?

Anya wasn't going to let that happen.

She sprinted toward Vermin, who was focused on shredding Miguel, and sent a few quick punches to his head, knocking the foul-smelling rat-guy backward. He was dazed, his cloudy red eyes at half-mast, drool dripping from his yellowed fangs. The respite gave

Miguel a chance to clamber to his feet. He shot two bursts of organic webbing into Vermin's monstrous eyes, then sent a quick jab to the villain's midsection, shunting him backward.

But whatever pause in the battle that brought was short-lived as Vermin flickered out of existence in a flash. Anya watched and could almost feel Traveller's attention moving, like a chess master choosing his next move.

She felt a breath catch in her mouth as she watched the red-tinged symbiote creature, Carnage, speed toward them—his left hand morphing into a scythe-like shape, a psychotic cackle coming from his mouth. Anya had heard horror stories about him. He may have been a figment of Traveller's mind, but it still looked and felt real.

"Hey, little girl, you all dressed up to play with us big boys?" Carnage said, his voice sounding like glass shattering. "Hope you like to hurt."

Anya didn't play into Carnage's hands. She'd dealt with plenty of bullies before—not just the ones that wore spandex or had super-powers. The one thing that they fed off was attention. And fear. Though she was scared, she wasn't going to let him see that.

"You got this," Miguel said as he shot a strand of

webbing toward Traveller. "I'll try to take out the central nervous system."

She nodded, turning her full attention to the serial killer with the alien embedded in his being. He was raising his blade hand, his giant maw of a mouth gaping open and hinting at a dark abyss within. Anya let him get within a few feet—then shot a few blasts of her own webbing at his legs, connecting and twisting her hands around the strands. At first, Carnage seemed confused, but then she tugged—knocking him backward and off-balance. It felt almost too easy, she thought.

"These are watered-down versions," Anya yelled to Miguel, who turned to listen. He was mid-swing, heading toward Traveller, who seemed to be straining under the pressure of managing so many different inventions. Perhaps it'd been easier before, she thought, when all he had to create were a bunch of Scriers that all looked and talked alike. But what was happening now was a bit more creative. "The more creations he throws at us, the harder it is on him. It's like he doesn't have the juice for it yet. And these versions don't match the real thing."

Or did they?

Just as Miguel was starting to turn his head back to focus on Traveller, to try to disrupt the linchpin of this whole charade, a giant, green gamma-hued fist knocked him away. Anya almost worried it'd sent him into orbit for a second. But Miguel, spinning around violently, was still able to shoot another web line to latch on to the edge of Valhalla's roof—avoiding a possibly fatal dip into the waters below.

"Seem . . . pretty real . . . to me," Miguel groaned as he pulled himself back up to his feet.

But by then, Anya was too occupied to be much help to Miguel.

"Anya Corazon, of the Spider Society," a black-robed woman said, flanked by two similarly dressed attackers. "We meet again. I wonder how you'll fare this time? Without the help of your dead mentor, eh?"

The words stung. They felt all too real to Anya. Either Judas Traveller's imitation of the Sisterhood of the Wasp was pitch-perfect or there was more to his role with them than she'd ever thought.

Anya, crouched down and poised for battle, felt her joints freeze. Felt her mind whir back to that night not so long ago when she'd witnessed another Miguel needlessly murdered. Someone who cared for her. Who'd taught her how to survive. These were the people that killed him, even if they weren't really. They were close enough. So why couldn't she move? she wondered.

A series of kicks landed—one to her face, spinning

her around, another in her midsection, sending her backward. By the end of it, she was on the ground, clutching her stomach, the taste of blood in her mouth, her vision hampered by a long crack down the left side of her goggles. She felt dizzy. Pain shooting through her. A tinge of the familiar nausea that accompanied the inevitable fading out of her powers.

But she wasn't going to quit now.

She thought she heard her bones creak as she wobbled to her feet. Caught a glimpse of the surprise on the main Wasp Society baddie's eyes. Maybe this wasn't going to be so easy for them, Anya thought.

"Another beating, then?" the woman said, stepping toward Anya. "Very well."

The lead Wasp took a swing, but this time Anya was ready—she ducked, feeling her opponent lurch forward unexpectedly. Anya sent her knee into the villain's rib cage, feeling a slight rush as the villain groaned in pain. Anya straightened up and jabbed her elbow into the Wasp Society leader's back. She didn't look down, the *thump* of her landing enough to let Anya know she was knocked out. The other two attackers seemed hesitant, confused. Anya looked past them to see Miguel grappling with Traveller. Traveller was distracted, she realized. When he was, even his most precise creations would falter.

She jumped up, sending a sweeping kick toward the two remaining thugs, knocking them back in one swift motion. But instead of landing, they faded mid-drop. She could see the other villains—the future Hulk, Vulture in mid-flight—scramble out of existence for a moment, before, by what seemed like sheer force of will, re-forming.

Her head started to spin again. Stronger this time. She felt the edges of her vision blur around her as nausea charged through her body. *Oh no,* she thought. *Not now. Not now . . .*

She felt the hands gripping her shoulder first, then felt her body being pulled back and tossed, the air around her speeding by as she slammed into the ground, her arms and legs skidding on the smooth roof, desperate for purchase. Her hand clutched at something, at last, as her body dangled over the edge— stories and stories of sky and air between her and what was sure to be a deadly landing, water or not. Her body swayed as she felt her fingers digging into the edge of the building, the one thing keeping her from something more final. The dizziness wasn't helping— disorienting, making it seem like she was swaying when she wasn't—up was down; she couldn't tell what was around her.

She closed her eyes, felt her body continue to sway,

but also felt some sense of calm overcome her. She took a deep breath. She heard the sounds of a scuffle—screaming, thuds, and *oomphs*—but kept her eyes closed. She knew her powers were flickering. But she could still feel something inside her. Felt the tattoo on her arm throbbing—slower but still there.

Her eyes fluttered open, and she pulled herself—slowly, but up. She vaulted over the small ledge and was on her feet. The Wasp Society's leader was looking the other way as her men seemed to pile onto Miguel, who was doing his best to dodge and weave, but was slowly being battered down. Anya didn't wait a second longer.

She reached out and grabbed the leader's hair, pulling her face to Anya's knee and hearing a satis-fying *krrk*—then letting her drop to the floor, a slight groan escaping her lips. The two other Wasp Society members looked at Anya, surprise on their faces as she stepped toward them.

She allowed herself a moment to scan the rooftop—the villains were gone, except for one shadowy figure that seemed to be approaching from the skies. She couldn't make it out. But she also couldn't see Traveller anywhere. The eerie quiet was unsettling, Anya thought.

The thunder came first. Then the crackle of light-ning took over the skies—which had gotten darker before becoming almost pitch-black. Anya heard the Wasp thugs skitter away; then the sound of their steps disappeared. She looked back to see Miguel slowly getting to his feet, his mask torn, his bruised face slightly visible under it. The men were gone; Traveller was gone. But something was happening.

"Thanks for scaring them off," Miguel said, stepping closer to Anya.

"Powers are about done. Not sure what I did. But something's coming," she said.

The shadowy figure, harder to see in the darkness, was still heading toward them, carried on the air on something. Anya thought she heard laughing, too.

"Where's Traveller?" she asked, her eyes still on the shape making a beeline for them.

Miguel pointed toward the far edge of the roof, across from them.

"Over there," he said. "He set up El Obelisco but created some kind of shield—he did something that blasted me here, in time to tangle with those Wasp goons. But he's there, under some protective spell. I can't see in, but I'm sure he can see out."

That's when Anya noticed it—the way the light reflected off a shape in a strange, unnatural way. As if a mirrored ball were positioned on the other side of

Valhalla, hiding in plain sight. But what was this *thing* heading toward them?

Miguel recognized it before she did.

"No . . . no," he said. "Not now."

"What is it?" Anya asked.

But by then the figure had gotten close enough to recognize—or at least see. It was a man, standing on a vulture-like glider, his body in a dark green suit, a manic, hysterical goblin's mask over his face. Anya had read about her fair share of goblins—they were the Spider-Heroes' opposite number in many ways, whether green, red, gray, hob, demonic, or whatever. But she'd never seen this one. He fit in with the future aesthetic of Miguel's world, where another piece clicked into place.

Miguel's brother.

"It's not real," Anya said quickly. "It's not him, Miguel."

But her words were lost by the sound of the Goblin's laugh as he landed his glider and removed his mask. Revealing a face that was so much like Miguel's it made Anya gasp.

"Hey, bro," the Goblin said. "Happy to see me?"

"Gab . . . Gabri . . ." Miguel said, his voice cracking. Anya's heart ached. Even under the partially torn mask, she could see Miguel's stricken expression. She barely knew this man, but she knew enough to see how badly seeing his brother cut at him, figment or not. "You're alive . . ."

Anya took a step between Miguel and the apparition purporting to be his brother turned baddie. She wasn't going to let him suffer like this if she could help it.

"It's not him, Miguel," she said firmly, looking at the faux Goblin. "You know that. It's something Traveller created. He knows where to hit you. Because he made that first cut. He corrupted the real Gabri. This isn't him."

"Oh, how would you know, Arañita?" the Goblin said. But his use of that name—her father's pet name for her—threw Anya off. *What does this thing know?* "What have you lost?"

The words stung—as if they were talking around things they both knew. But what did the Goblin—or Traveller—know of what she'd lost? *Who* she'd lost?

Mami.

"Quit with the head games," Anya said, doubling down. "I'll break you if I have to."

She could still hear Miguel behind her, his breathing heavy. She felt a cold sheen of sweat form on her skin as she watched the Goblin's face begin to change— begin to contort. What was happening? The color of the mask morphed, just as the costume itself seemed to become something else, a different shape—a different person.

Anya already felt unsettled, but she only felt this more as she started to recognize details about what the Goblin was becoming, *who* the Goblin was becoming.

"Anya . . . what are you doing?"

The voice. Her mami's voice. But . . . but how?

"It's me, Anya," the creature—her mother—said. She looked older but had the same kind eyes, soft smile that Anya remembered. Anya wanted to believe it. "I've been waiting so long to see you. Why didn't you look for me, Arañita?"

This time, it was Miguel's turn. He stepped in front of Anya, spreading his arms to prevent her from sidestepping him.

"You're not real. That Goblin isn't real, either," he said, his voice seething. "This is a trick. An evil trick perpetrated by an evil man who can't just leave things be. Go away."

"Away? I have been away," Anya's mother said, looking almost incredulous. "I'm back now, though. Back to see my daughter. What a wonderful woman she's become . . ."

Anya was shaken out of her hypnotic reverie as Miguel's webbing landed on the creature's mouth, blocking her from saying more things that sounded like Anya's mami. Anya felt torn—she wanted to talk to her, to learn where her mami had been. But she also knew this *was* a trick—a cruel joke to delay them. Anya felt her heart breaking as she stepped toward the impostor.

"You're a fraud," Anya said. "My mami would never leave me. Something happened to her. This isn't it."

The creature morphed again, her mami's hands now becoming claws, ripping the webbing off. Her mami's face was now something else, too—a pale, vampiric shape, long black hair framing the face of a man she only recognized from the book Miguel had shown her.

"This *is* it, young one," the creature said, taking on the shape of Morlun, his voice low and gravel-laced. "Do you think everything happens in a vacuum, apart from itself? You and your foolish new friend are just blips to me. To my eventual awakening. Your potential—the good you would've done, could've done— that's what feeds me. What will open the gates for me. If you think all of your tragedies were just a series of unfortunate events, then you truly know nothing, and have . . . no hope—"

The Morlun creature was disrupted by a fierce punch to the face, and Anya felt herself take a few

steps back as Miguel sent another series of swings at the
monster, which was slowly morphing into . . . nothing?
Its shape was losing form, and the sounds it was emit-
ting would haunt Anya for some time. But as it stood
now, the creature was nothing. Just a blob-like thing, a
punching bag for Miguel O'Hara and his pent-up rage.

"Not him," Miguel said, sending another flurry of
punches. "Not him . . . not her . . . not anyone . . .
garbage . . . not a person . . ."

Anya placed a hand on Miguel's arm, gently.

"Stop, Miguel," she said, her voice calm. "It's not
real."

Miguel did stop, panting heavily. He yanked his
mask off, and Anya could see the pain in his eyes, his
face streaked with tears, his jaw battered.

"I didn't want this," he said. "No one was hurting
me anymore. I couldn't hurt anyone again."

She started to say something but stopped. He wasn't
done yet.

"But I was hiding. I was pretending to be alive,"
Miguel said, his eyes widening. "Now I know, though.
That's what he wanted. From me. From us. To keep us
down so he could do what he wanted to do. Drain us.
Abuse us. Hurt us. Use the lives we could've saved—
the good we could've done—for his own dark purposes.
Not anymore."

He tossed the ratty mask to the floor and pulled a new one from inside his costume. He placed it on his head.

"You carry a spare?" Anya asked.

Miguel gave her a quick thumbs up. *Of course he does,* Anya thought.

"Watch out, Traveller," he said. "We're coming for you."

Anya smiled.

———

They approached the sphere cautiously—light reflecting and refracting from the surface of the shield, lightning and the moon's reflection visible on the pliable shape.

"This is weird," Anya said.

"I would say that's accurate," Miguel said, a few steps ahead of her. "What's he doing in there?"

"Only one way to find out," Anya said.

"No, wait—"

But Anya ignored his warning, charging toward the mirrored shape. Even with her powers on the fritz, she could still feel when her strength was intact, and this was as good as she was going to feel for a long time, she realized. She barreled into the structure, shoulder-first, feeling it give way slightly, feeling more like something organic than steel or concrete.

She backed up, braced herself, and charged again. This time she felt it give way a bit more, the surface of the mirror structure almost bending backward. She felt another *thud* next to her. Miguel. He was pushing, too. The sphere seemed to strain under the pressure—a slight hissing sound coming from inside. Then, suddenly, it fully gave way, and Anya felt herself tumble forward—and through? She squinted her eyes to adapt to the light—bright, all over. She could make out a figure, standing before something large and inert. El Obelisco—droning with a power Anya hadn't witnessed before. It seemed to be . . . *vibrating*?

She heard Miguel land next to her. Then the figure turned, and Anya could make out Traveller—his eyes looking more manic than ever before. She noticed the lights—not just the brightness, but the streams of orange and green bouncing around the mirrored pod Traveller had created, energetic bursts electrifying whatever they touched, crackling with power. Something was happening.

"Again with you two," Traveller said, shaking his head, like an irked hall monitor in a junior high school. "Sometimes I wonder if you *do* have a death wish."

"It's over, Traveller," Miguel said, getting to his feet. "We won't let you go back. It ends here."

"Over? My, even after an extended break, you still

have your hero patter down—how charming," Traveller said, still focused on El Obelisco, which seemed to be shaking almost violently now, the orange-and-green energies crackling off it and forming a single blast of power—connecting directly with Traveller's hands, causing the older man to vibrate, too. "But things are far from over, you fool. In fact, I'd wager they've just begun."

And, in an instant, the colorful energies dancing around the cramped space seemed to coalesce, creating a single, blinding blast that enveloped them all.

Anya felt a shock of pain through her entire being, followed by nothing—just darkness.

CHAPTER 25

Where the hell's Robertson? I'm hearing rumors
Spider-Man is off-planet fighting some kind
of . . . secret war? Can't we get a reporter to
confirm that? Brant—get Joe in here, now!"

The scream seemed to echo through Anya's skull—
moments before she opened her eyes, the din of a
crowded, bustling newsroom filling the burst of quiet
she'd felt before things went black. She felt Miguel next
to her, shaking his head, disoriented. Their eyes met
just a moment before they noticed everyone around
them—they were in an office of some kind, and they
were definitely not in the future, Anya realized. But
was that a good thing?

The crowd of people—reporters, editors, staff,
visitors—all seemed to turn to them in unison, looks of
fear, concern, and panic on their faces. If this was New
York, *her* New York, Anya knew its citizens were jaded
when it came to things like teleportation, time travel,
and massive destruction—but even then, it was probably just something they read on the news, not what

they experienced firsthand. Not surprisingly, most of
the people seemed to be taking cautious steps backward. All except one.

The man, older, gruff, wearing a very out-of-date
mustache and a buzz cut that had gone out of style
before Kennedy was president, walked—no, *sauntered*—
to them, an unlit cigar hanging from his mouth. He
looked defiant and . . . annoyed?

"What in the world are you Halloween rejects doing
in my newsroom?" the man said. Anya finally put a
name to the face—it was J. Jonah Jameson, publisher of
the *Daily Bugle*. She knew the man by reputation mostly.
Seen him on TV, too. Heard her papi talk about how
difficult he was and how he hated having to work for a
man like that. She missed her papi. "Can't you freaks
see I have a paper to put out?"

He was waving a stack of newspapers at them, as
if he were swatting at a pesky fly, swinging the stack
closer with each word.

"How many Spider-weirdos are there these days,
anyway?" Jameson said. "Didn't you get the memo?
Your fearless leader is gone! Wasn't one godforsaken
wall-crawler enough?"

She heard Miguel groan behind her.

"Oh man, we're *here*?" he said. "We gotta get out—
and fast, kid."

"I agree," Anya said before turning to look at Jameson. "You're Jonah Jameson, right?"

Sputtering a bit, Jameson responded.

"Uh, yeah, of course—yes, I am," he said.

"Someone I care about says you talk too much," Anya said. She felt one good thing, standing here. Her powers seemed to be back. She took advantage, sending a quick burst of webbing into Jonah's face, covering his mouth. "Maybe you should fix that."

As Jameson struggled with the webbing that abruptly silenced him, Anya and Miguel made for a nearby window—in a rather large office, loaded with awards and pictures of Jameson with celebrities from every corner of the city—and jumped out into the smoky, crusty New York City air. How she'd missed this place.

But were they back? she wondered as she and Miguel clambered up a nearby office building, finding a relatively quiet spot on the roof. From what she could tell, this was *her* New York. The sounds, smells, and sights seemed familiar. But even though she was a relatively green super hero, she knew enough about alternate universes, timelines, and doppelgängers to be wary.

She watched as Miguel pulled back his sleeve to reveal a tiny wristband. He tapped it with a finger. Immediately, a miniature version of his holo-assistant, Lyla, appeared.

"Hello, Miguel," she said, smiling, as if he were just calling to check in. "I see you're time-traveling again."

"Been a rough day, Lyla," he said.

"Still look good in that suit," she said with a brief wink.

Miguel sighed.

"Lyla, we need help," he said, sounding annoyed and amused all at once. "Where the shock are we?"

Anya leaned over Miguel's shoulder to get a closer look at the display coming from Miguel's wrist.

"Wow, dude."

"What?" he asked, turning to face her.

"You keep your assistant in your wristwatch?" Anya asked. "Is it like a fancy step-counter thing?"

"Step counter?"

"Never mind," she said.

Miguel's wrist chirped, and they both turned to watch Lyla.

"It appears you're back in Anya's time—a few days after her initial disappearance—"

Before Lyla could continue, Anya interjected with an anxious yelp.

"Oh no, ohmygod, ohmygod, Papi is going to be losing his mind, he probably thinks I'm dead," she said, skittering to her feet and looking around, as if hoping to find a speed-rail ride to Brooklyn. "I gotta go, gotta go."

She leapt into the air, shooting a strand of webbing and hoping for the best. Within a moment, she was out of earshot, and all Miguel could do was try to keep pace. Lyla watched from her perch on his wrist, a smirk on her face.

"I'm glad you're making friends, Miguel," Lyla said.

Miguel, between web swings, tapped his wrist—shutting mini Lyla off. He smiled underneath his mask. He was glad, too, he realized.

CHAPTER 26

She made it to Fort Greene in about fifteen minutes, managing to sneak into her room, swipe some clothes, and sneak out without disturbing anyone. But her stomach was churning. She had to think, think, think.

Her papi, Gilberto, was probably shaken to his core—a few years after losing his wife, now his daughter had been missing for days. What was she going to tell him? Where could she have been?

She didn't have time to decide. As she approached the steps to her apartment building—she saw him and immediately ran.

"Papi!" she yelled.

Gilberto turned, panic and then relief in his eyes as Anya stumbled into his arms. They clutched each other tightly. She could smell his cologne, feel his bristly beard on her cheek. Her eyes watered as she and her papi hugged. She knew Judas Traveller was still out there. Knew that the universe was still at risk. But for right now, in this moment, she felt safe and at home.

But the feeling was short-lived. Gilberto pulled back for a moment. She could see his eyes were red, and his expression had gone from one of surprise to concern—and anger.

"Arañita, where in the world have you been?" he said, his tone becoming heated. "Are you hurt? Hungry? I thought we'd lost you. Just like we'd lost—"

He didn't let himself finish the sentence, instead pulling Anya in for another hug, tighter this time, if that were even possible. Then the sobbing started, his face buried in her neck, short, powerful cries that she could have never imagined. She started to get a sense of the dark thoughts that must have run through Gilberto's mind as he stayed up to all hours, waiting for Anya to return, or for news of her fate. All the deadly possibilities that could have closed that loop. She felt a great sense of shame and despair. Why couldn't she just *tell him*? she thought. Why must she keep this a secret?

"I need to know, Anya," Gilberto said between stilted sobs. "I need to know what happened."

She would tell him, she decided, then and there. It wasn't worth the secret. It wasn't worth not knowing her own father—or not allowing him to know her and her life, as he'd known all this time.

She was tired of this secret life—of changing in dark corners, coming home late, and pretending she was living a normal teen existence. Especially when it required her to hide everything from the one person in the world who'd earned her absolute trust. Gilberto Corazon was no stranger to danger, to fighting for the truth. He was an intrepid investigative reporter. In a matter of time, he'd probably figure Anya's activities out himself, anyway.

"Papi, I need to talk . . . to tell you—"

Before she could finish, she heard someone approaching up the steps to the entryway of their apartment building.

She wasn't sure if her papi saw the flicker of recognition that crossed her face as she saw Miguel, wearing some sharp aviator shades and dressed in a very modern suit and tie, walking toward them.

"It seems, Mr. Corazon, that your daughter was caught up in a high-end theft of some kind," Miguel said. He was walking . . . differently. With a confidence Anya hadn't seen before. But what was he doing?

Miguel extended a hand. Gilberto took it hesitantly.

"Miguel O'Hara," he said. "NYPD, Special Crimes Unit."

Gilberto nodded, but Anya could see in his eyes something was up. Something wasn't clicking in his head.

"Looks like someone swiped that artifact your

daughter went to see a few nights back," Miguel said. "In the process, your daughter was captured, too. She's a smart kid, though. Managed to get free, not that much worse for wear. We intercepted her near where we think the stolen item is being held."

Gilberto cleared his throat, his eyes narrowing slightly.

"I don't know who you are, Mr. O'Hara," he said, drawing out his words slowly. "But there's no Special Crimes Unit in the NYPD."

Anya stiffened. Her papi was smart. She appreciated Miguel's effort, but—

"It's a secret, pop," Miguel said with a smile. "That's what makes it special."

Gilberto started to respond but stopped as Miguel crouched down slightly to Anya's eye level.

"Anya, you're very tough—very brave," Miguel said. "We are going to get the people that did this. I just want you and your dad to know . . . you're a hero. You're a very special person."

Then he leaned and gave Anya a hug. She didn't know what to do at first, but after a moment, she returned the embrace—and the meaning behind it.

"And the Oscar goes to . . ." Anya whispered to Miguel quickly. She felt his hand slide a small slip of paper into hers.

Anya pulled back as Miguel stood up. They nodded at each other, and Miguel gave her a quick wink before turning to wave at Gilberto.

As he watched Miguel walk away from their building, Gilberto spoke, his voice starting to crack with emotion.

"I don't know what the hell just happened, Arañita," he said, his hand clutching her shoulder. "But I am glad you're here. That you're safe."

He pulled her into another long hug.

"I don't know what I'd do without you."

CHAPTER 27

Anya stepped back from the hug, wiping her own tears from her eyes.

"Papi, I need to sleep. I need to rest," she said. She wasn't lying. She *was* dead tired. But she also had Miguel's note burning a hole in her pocket. "Is that okay?"

"Of course, mija," he said, leading her into the building and walking toward their apartment. "Get some sleep. I'll be here when you wake up."

Anya felt dazed as she walked through her apartment's living room—as if shambling through a dream. Everything was where she'd left it, but felt off, distant. Her papi's makeshift office on the dining room table. Her stack of books by the door. A collection of family photos on the entertainment center. After battling imaginary villains and literally jumping through time, nothing felt real. Solid. She was unmoored—like she was imagining her life somehow.

"You're tired," she mumbled to herself as she

opened the door to her bedroom, the same Taylor Swift poster hanging over her bed. The same stack of true-crime books on her nightstand. It was all where it needed to be. She closed the door behind her and let herself drop onto her unmade bed.

She just wanted to drift off to sleep, to leave Traveller and super villains and other problems to the real heroes. But she knew she couldn't do that. She was a hero herself, whether she wanted to be or not. And now it was Miguel's turn to be trapped in another time. She couldn't just leave him to his own devices. He was rusty. The reality was, they had to save the world now. Together. Whether they wanted to or not.

She pulled the tiny sheet of paper from her back pocket and unfolded it slowly, knowing that the second she did, she'd be on the clock. She let herself savor the final seconds of normalcy, of just being Anya Corazon, high school student and daughter to Gilberto, before she'd be Araña, teenage crimefighter, again.

The note was written in a stilted, thoughtful scrawl. Guess Miguel wasn't used to writing by hand, she thought. Neither was she, if she thought about it.

The note read:

Hey, kid.

   Hope your dad buys my story. Only had a few minutes to cook it up. If not, like any good lie, it'll create just enough doubt to give you some time to craft your own take.

I've got a lead on Traveller. But I need your help. I need a favor. Stay home. Stay safe. My gut says that if I destroy El Obelisco, your powers will return for good. Our trapped potential will come back. What does that mean? Not sure, really. But I think, somehow, you coming to my time threw a wrench in Traveller's plans for me. It woke me up. You disrupted him, and that's a debt I—the world—can never repay.

But for now, it's too big a risk for you. Traveller is no joke, and he's out to not only destroy us, and heroes like us—but erase us from existence to bring Morlun back. The best thing you can do is sit tight and be with your dad. I'm sure he's happy you're home.

I also wanted to say thank you. In case I don't see you again. I'm not an emotional guy (shocker!), or one for sad good-byes— but you've shown me a lot over the last few days. I may not want to wear this suit, but I need to. Whether I want to be one, I am a hero. You taught me that, and I can never truly repay you. If Traveller's mission is to absorb and destroy the good we're doing— to convince us we don't belong, that we're not fit to wear these costumes and do good—then he's already failed. That's thanks to you. You have a ton of heart, Anya, powers or not. I think my brother would've liked you.

Stay safe. I'll see you somewhere, sometime.

Abrazos,

Miguel

Anya looked at the note for another few moments. She could feel the tears welling up in her eyes. She could also feel an anger boiling inside her.

She liked Miguel. She really did. But he was wrong. She wasn't going to sit this one out.

"Guess you don't know me all that well, Miggy," she said, leaping off her bed and digging out the spare costume she'd tucked underneath it. She started to suit up. "Heroes don't quit when their powers go haywire. Heroes are heroes, period. No matter what."

CHAPTER 28

Gwen Stacy lived for days like these.

Boring days. Days where all she had to do was go to her next class at Empire State University and just . . . be. Be normal. Be calm. Do her thing.

She liked boring because her life had been anything but. Her world had been anything but, really. Here she was, on another *Earth*—a world kinda like her own, but also very different. See, on her world, she was bitten by a radioactive spider and granted amazing powers. On this Earth, well—that happened to someone else. Someone she cared about back home. A man named Peter Parker. On her world, Peter Parker had died after a throwdown battle. Gwen still struggled with her part in it all. Like the Peter Parker of this world, Gwen had taken on a heroic mantle—wearing a cool costume and everything. She'd also realized that with great power came equally great responsibilities. So when not trying to get her degree or keep her life in order, she was often leaping between rooftops as Ghost-Spider. It was the opposite of boring.

Which is why she appreciated today, she thought as she walked out of the main entrance of ESU's student union. Today, she'd just go to class, grab lunch, then maybe even take a nap. Catch up with some friends. Heck, she might even get to watch some TV before bed. Nice, quiet, and—

She stopped short when she saw the man. She felt the familiar buzzing in the back of her head—her spider-sense, a red flag warning her of danger. It seemed to really be in overdrive now. She braced herself as the man made his way toward her.

"Gwendolyn Stacy," the man said, his long gray hair almost floating around his face. He was wearing a long coat, and his eyes looked supercharged and wild, a strange orange-and-green aura surrounded him.

"Who are you?" Gwen asked.

"Gwen," the man said, hoarsely repeating her name as he raised a hand in her direction. "It is time for you to help me . . . to help my cause. It's time for another Spider's potential to be sacrificed for the greater evil. Will you help?"

Gwen tilted her head.

"Getting a real stranger-danger vibe here," she said, raising her fists. "Even if you seem to know who I am. So, either we talk or we fight—what's your choice?"

CHAPTER 29

Just as Anya slid her Araña goggles over her eyes, things started to get really weird.

First it was her phone. It was buzzing every minute. Not with concerned texts from her friends, wondering where she'd been. No. They were *Bugle* news alerts. Chaos downtown. Fires in Queens. Wreckage in Bed-Stuy.

She flipped open her Neighborhood Watch app. She wasn't sure how other super heroes did it, but she used this crowdsourced application a lot. People from all over uploaded videos, pictures, or just comments about crimes in progress. A third of them were crap, but every once in a while, you got something real. Something dangerous.

This was one of those times.

Whatever Judas Traveller was doing, it was out of control. And Anya wasn't sure he could backtrack from it.

She scrolled through the app's news feed—her eyes

widening at each picture. She saw what looked like
World War II soldiers storming Staten Island. The
long-dead first Green Goblin tossing a pumpkin bomb
in Union Square. The original X-Men battling someone named the Vanisher near SoHo. The Lizard and a
bleached werewolf creature named Man-Wolf brawling
on the BQE. She had to stop herself. This was bad.

She slid her phone in her pocket. She had to find
Miguel. She had to figure out where to snag Traveller
and stop this madness. Had Traveller somehow kicked
El Obelisco into overdrive? Had that caused some kind
of irreparable rift in time? Anya was no scientist, but it
seemed like people who shouldn't be around were very
much around and wrecking the place while they were
at it. She opened her bedroom window and started to
climb out when she heard a voice behind her.

"Anya? ¿Qué haces, mijita?"

That voice.

Anya turned around. There was no one there. The
voice had sprung out of thin air.

Mami's voice. Her mother was . . . here?

"Mami?" Anya said. She could hear the quiver in
her own voice as she stepped farther into her room,
which felt very cold now.

"Stay here, Anya," the voice said, clearer now—but

where was it coming from? "Tenemos que hablar, Arañita. Stay here."

Anya froze.

How could she go anywhere?

The pumpkin bomb whizzed past Miguel's head, exploding on the building behind him—sending pieces in every direction. He ducked to avoid the shards as he shot another strand of webbing—trying to keep his momentum going. Trying to get to where he needed to go.

He could hear the evil laughing behind him, getting louder. He glanced back for a second—saw the green-and-purple figure; the large, unblinking eyes; the endless, terrifying grin. What the hell was it with goblins and spiders? he thought. This wasn't Gabri, thankfully, but it wasn't good. Miguel still felt out of sync—his timing slightly off, the moves that used to come instinctively now requiring a second or two of thought. That could cost him.

He knew Peter Parker, the Spider-Man of this time. They'd fought battles together. Saved the universe once or twice, too. He knew how deadly this—*his*—Green Goblin was, especially this iteration. The original. A businessman named Norman Osborn, juiced up by a super-serum of his own creation. The only downside was that the serum drove him power-mad. Slight defect, Miguel mused as he pulled himself up, avoiding another pumpkin bomb.

"You're not Parker, but you'll have to do," the Green Goblin said, his voice a high-pitch screech. "One dead Spider is better than none, eh?"

Another bomb. Another dodge. But Miguel wasn't sure how long he could keep this up. The Goblin was good—strong, quick, and hell-bent on not just beating Miguel, but obliterating him. And Miguel had to get around him if he was to have any shot at stopping Traveller.

The Goblin pointed a finger at him, which, for a moment, Miguel thought was odd—until a blast of laser fire was emitted from the purple glove. Miguel tried to dodge, but the shot connected with his back and threw him off-balance. He lost his grip on his webbing and felt himself falling. He heard the Goblin exclaim, "That was too easy!"

Miguel cursed under his breath as he reached his arms out, trying to latch on to anything, the tiny pincerlike claws on his hands scraping for purchase. He couldn't die like this, he thought. Just as he'd rediscovered why he put on the suit in the first place. He could see the Goblin, perched on his devilish-looking glider, swirling above him—getting smaller and smaller.

No. It won't end like this, Miguel. He stretched his arms out farther, catching some of the building with a free hand. Felt his fingers dig into the concrete. Deeper. His body's momentum was diverted, and he had to position his legs to stop himself from crashing into the building. But he did it.

The Goblin's appearance had thrown Miguel off after his meeting with Anya. According to Lyla, there was a temporal vortex of sorts forming near a college in the area, Empire State University. Which led Miguel to believe that Traveller was using the area as his ad hoc base of operations. But why? He wasn't sure.

Miguel knew that Traveller wanted to disable as many Spider-Heroes as possible and drain them of their potential. Traveller would basically redirect the good the heroes would've done if they'd stayed in costume back into El Obelisco. Somehow, the ancient device would, in turn, amplify Traveller's powers. If Traveller's powers got strong enough, he'd be able to reactivate Morlun.

Morlun, a centuries-old psychic vampire who Traveller seemed to think was as close to pure evil as possible, was of great interest to the gray-haired villain. For Traveller, a student of evil and all its power, the chance to not only study, but to serve under a being of pure, unbridled evil was probably akin to winning the bad-guy lottery. So, anything that put his plan at risk was a big problem. Were Miguel and Anya having some kind of effect—causing Traveller to spin out of control? It seemed like that to Miguel. Had he and Anya, hitchhiking back to this time, added some urgency to the villain's plans? Miguel wondered.

Either way, they couldn't—he couldn't—let Traveller summon a creature of Morlun's powers. It could prove devastating not only to present-day New York, but to the entire timestream. In his efforts to disable Miguel, Anya, and perhaps others, Traveller had jumped around in time—manipulating Miguel's brother, Gabriel, and, from what Miguel could discern, Anya's life as well—murdering Miguel Legar, a mentor of sorts, and—

His thought was derailed by the Green Goblin—who'd woven around the building, catching Miguel by surprise.

Miguel felt the Goblin's hands clamp around his neck, pulling him backward. The villain's strong fingers tightening into his windpipe.

Miguel had had enough. He reached behind him, claws at the ready, and swiped freely. He felt his sharp fingertips slicing through the cloth of the Goblin's mask, then deeper into the flesh of the villain's face. Miguel felt some relief as the Goblin released him and squealed in surprise. He also had to admit he felt a little jolt of satisfaction.

He tried to create some space between himself and the Goblin, watching as the villain, still on his glider, spiraled around, screaming in pain, his hands clutching his tattered mask.

Miguel also knew enough, from the limited information available on the Heroic Age, that Norman Osborn—the original Green Goblin—didn't look like this anymore. The version Miguel was seeing seemed more akin to the way he looked the first time Osborn had put on the costume, before his apparent death and eventual return. The files on this era were confusing and often contradictory. Still, it made Miguel wonder if he wasn't facing another Traveller creation. But that could pose a bigger problem.

"You cut me . . . You shredded my face," the Goblin screamed, speeding toward Miguel on his Goblin Glider, his cheeks bloodied and his eyes enraged. "For that, you'll pay. Parker or not, I'll have your heart."

"I don't have time for this," Miguel said, shooting two strands of webbing at the Goblin, both hitting him squarely in the face, covering his anger-fueled eyes. The temporary delaying tactic only served to enrage the Goblin further, but that was the idea. "I have places to go, Normie."

Miguel tugged back on the strands of webbing, yanking the Goblin off his glider and swinging him into a nearby building—hard. Then he did it again, heaving him across the street into another building, the loud *thunk* a sign that the Goblin hadn't been able to avoid the crash and was unconscious. He watched as the purple-and-green villain started to slide down the side of the skyscraper. Miguel felt a jolt of panic. Monstrous villain or not, he couldn't let him die. But was this Norman Osborn even . . . real?

The answer came quickly—as the Goblin seemed to fizzle out of existence, leaving an empty space in his place.

"Huh," Miguel said.

The Goblin's disappearance confirmed for Miguel that the situation was all Traveller's doing—but this villain also struck him as different from the previous set of Traveller creations. Tougher. More focused. As if Traveller was not only getting better at spreading his powers over great distances—but also stronger. That was bad.

Miguel needed help. He was certain of that. He

refused to put Anya in danger anymore, though. The kid deserved to be with her dad, at home, trying to be normal.

But isn't that what Traveller wants? Miguel thought. He shook his head. No. There had to be another way. Miguel could do this. Alone.

He shot another strand of webbing toward his destination: Empire State University.

Gwen Stacy climbed up the side of the ESU Science Building and wondered how often Peter Parker had days like this. Y'know, moments where old, long-haired dudes walked up to him while he was dressed in his secret identity, talking about Spider potential and sacrifice. Real creeper stuff, bold and italicized. She'd talked tough in the moment, but her brain won out over her guts. A few backflips later and she was able to dart into an empty science lab to suit up, all proper like. If there was gonna be a throwdown, she mused, she needed to look the part.

As she peeked over the edge of the building, though, she wondered if she should've just kept running.

Gwen knew Empire State University had a lot of students. She was used to weaving through packed hallways and scrambling to find a seat when she was a minute late to class. But this . . . this was not what she'd anticipated when this universe's Peter Parker told her "things could get crowded."

Here she was, on the roof of the ESU Science Building, wearing her familiar Ghost-Spider togs, surrounded by some skeletal-looking creeps called Scriers and a familiar face—a green-furred bad guy known as the Jackal, who seemed to be in charge.

When that old creep Traveller approached her, Gwen had made a swift exit—her spider-sense sounding the alarm. But then she discovered that these Scriers—and this retro version of the Jackal—were hot on her trail. She'd managed to find a moment to change into her Ghost-Spider duds—barely. Even being from another universe, she still had some semblance of a secret identity, and it wouldn't help her rep to be chased by these apparitions through the halls of her school. But that seemed to be the least of her problems now.

"Gwen Stacy, as I live and breathe," the Jackal said in a sharp, singsong voice. The Scriers were grouped at either side of him, waiting to charge. "When Traveller brought me in on this, he didn't mention you'd be involved."

"Back off, furball, I don't have time for this," Gwen said, leaping toward her attackers. If she'd learned one thing as a super hero, it was that you didn't wait to play defense. Sometimes you needed to take things into your own hands. "I don't know who this Trav—"

Her words were cut short, an electric shock shooting through her entire system. She fell to the ground with a loud *thud*, her head spinning. She looked up and saw a familiar shadow looming over her. Traveller.

"Normally, my dear, I'd use my abilities to try and win you over. Talk you out of this Spider nonsense. But that time has passed. And, to be honest," Traveller said, leaning down, his eyes on Gwen's, "I just don't need your potential all that badly."

He straightened up and motioned to the other side of the roof. Gwen followed his movement, her neck aching from the motion. She saw those weirdos—the Scriers—lugging a giant, smooth chunk of metal and stone toward her. It looked . . . super old? But it also seemed to be glowing with neon-green-and-orange energies. Not just glowing, but bursting with it. As if it was about to overload itself.

"What is that?"

"That, my dear, is a means to an end. My path to understanding the ultimate evil," Traveller continued, his voice rising in anticipation. "To serving the one true evil that I've longed to establish. With just a bit more energy, it will revive a being I have long worshipped. That's where you come in."

"You're insane."

"Oh, very much so," Traveller said with a dismissive nod. "But that's part of the fun, isn't it?"

"How did you know where to find me? To find us?" Gwen asked, incredulous. "I mean, this whole secret-identity thing is a big deal."

Traveller scoffed.

"I study evil, my dear," he said, a tinge of surprise on his face. "And a lifetime ago, I learned who wears the mask of your fabled Spider-Man. Figuring out the rest just took a little legwork. But you all didn't make it very hard for me, either."

"He'll stop you," Gwen spat. "Even if you knock me out, Spider-Man will stop you."

Traveller opened his mouth, not in surprise, but in glee. His head jerked back, a loud, cacophonous laugh spiraling out. It was unlike anything Gwen had ever heard. Wild, unhinged, and very, very sure of itself.

"Stop me?" Traveller said. "There's nothing to stop, Gwendolyn. The die is cast. Plus, young Parker is otherwise entangled—on some kind of off-world problem. By the time he realizes something is wrong here, it'll be too late—and the entire timeline will be ripped asunder, remade in the image of true evil: Morlun."

"Mor-whom?" Gwen asked. She followed the question by sticking out her tongue. Hey, if this super-hero game couldn't be fun—why bother? Traveller struck her as the kind of guy who didn't like being trolled. "Never heard of him."

Traveller frowned. He wasn't big on humor, apparently.

Gwen noticed some more motion on the other side of the roof—another batch of Scriers was moving something else. Not as big as the giant old piece of whatever. No, but much creepier. Some kind of container. Was it a casket? Gwen blinked a few times. The coffin was being wheeled in front of the other, giant device. With some effort, the Scriers opened the sarcophagus—and Gwen caught a glimpse of something terrifying, the evil and danger pulsing out of the long box.

Inside was a large figure, tall, powerful, his long black hair slicked back, revealing his chalk-white skin. Gwen didn't need a doctorate to figure out who it was: Morlun. The figure looked gigantic—and she knew he wasn't just your run-of-the-mill, spandex-wearing baddie. He was a force of nature. Odds were definitely not in her favor. Nope, nope, nope.

"Your humor doesn't even succeed at delaying us, impetuous child. The time is upon us," Traveller said, glancing at the giant device—which had begun to glow even more forcefully once Morlun's casket was placed in front of it. "With just one more Spider, Morlun will rise—and all of the timestream will be his . . . and mine!"

"That . . . does not seem ideal," Gwen said to herself.

She started to say something else, but the words were drowned out by the roar of the crowd—a collection of Scriers, closing in on Gwen, their hands raised in anger, their mouths wailing in a unified victory cheer. Gwen had never been more scared in her life.

CHAPTER 30

The Green Goblin had just been a primer, Miguel realized as he caught sight of what was happening at Empire State University. Everything else was a distraction. Diversions meant to keep Miguel and the others all at bay while Traveller focused on his big plan: reviving Morlun. Miguel didn't like facing the reality that he was late to the main event.

He tried to pick up the pace, pulling himself along, despite his sore shoulder and the black eye he felt forming under his mask. The Green Goblin had done a number on him, if he was being honest, and he was far from being in peak form. He was off his game. He was hesitant. He was tired and just wanted to be home. But he was also as close to a last shot as one could be, and he was sick of Judas Traveller, Morlun, and everything Traveller had caused in his quest to awaken this ancient evil.

From Miguel's vantage point, he could see a swarm of Traveller's black-veiled thugs, the Scriers, surrounding a young woman dressed in a Spider-like outfit—white, pink, and black. She looked familiar, but Miguel couldn't pinpoint who she was. It was tough to keep track of them all, he thought. Whoever she was, she was in big trouble, and if Green Goblin was an example of Traveller's amped-up power set, these Scriers were probably a lot more dangerous than the flimsy ones he and Anya had faced off against in the future.

As he got closer, he could see the woman was holding her own. Her power set seemed similar to Parker's— she seemed to feel when someone was approaching, and her agility was mind-boggling. But she was over-whelmed, outnumbered. Even if Miguel made it to her in time, there was no guarantee they'd win.

Then Miguel looked at the other end of the roof, and his heart sank. There it was, El Obelisco, orange-and-green power swirling around it like some kind of paranormal tornado, getting stronger and bigger with each passing second. But that wasn't what sent a chill through Miguel—it was the coffin that was propped up in front of it, being held by a handful of Scriers who were looking into the light with dim, glazed stares. Miguel didn't need to see inside the casket to know who was in there, and how problematic it would be if he got out.

He landed on the roof just as the energies swirl-ing around El Obelisco seemed to coalesce, forming a single blast. As if on cue, the Scriers attacking the woman parted, leaving her open to attack. The energy hit her in the back, and from what Miguel could tell, it was not painless. She screamed, a mix of surprise and anguish. Miguel watched as the artifact increased the pressure on the woman and in turn sent another blast into the coffin. Miguel had taken a few steps toward the coffin when he saw something move.

No, not something. Someone.

He froze in his tracks as he watched the hulking figure of Morlun step out of the coffin. Morlun glanced at Miguel as he turned and walked toward the fallen woman. The Scriers, their job apparently complete, slowly faded from existence. There was another crea-ture, a furry green guy with big ears, Miguel noticed. He seemed to be bobbing and weaving around the fallen woman.

"Let me have her, Morlun," he said, his voice jolly but also laced with malice. "You're back. You don't need her, do you? Do you? Let Miles—"

Morlun raised an arm and snapped a finger in the creature's direction. A second later, the green crea-ture was gone, a pile of ash where it once stood. The woman, still reeling from the artifact's blast, raised an arm—as if that could stop Morlun.

The ancient creature spoke aloud, his voice low, echoing across the New York City rooftop.

"Your creations are no longer needed, Judas Traveller," Morlun said, still looking down at the woman. "I am here now. I have need of those powers, drawn from the good these beings would create. They are wasted on distractions—watered-down copies of people who would never come close to attaining the power and exalted stature of Morlun."

Miguel watched as Morlun crouched down, the movement almost gentle in its execution, but also frightening, coming from someone so dangerous. He gently lifted the woman's face toward him, two long, pale fingers on her chin. She looked back at him, defiant. Miguel liked this hero. He'd do whatever he could to save her. Starting now.

"Step away from her," Miguel said, his voice loud and forceful. "She's not alone."

Morlun turned to look at Miguel, the way someone might glance at an ant walking across their picnic blanket. A soft smile appeared on his face.

"Ah, yes. The washed-up Spider-Man of the future, finally back in action," Morlun said, straightening up and stepping toward Miguel. "How quaint of you. The retired failed hero puts on his uniform one more time to save the universe. That doesn't always end well, does it?"

Miguel glanced over to El Obelisco and noticed Traveller scurrying over to Morlun, mouth agape, arms outstretched.

"It has happened! The moment I've been dreaming of!" Traveller said, sounding desperate and giddy. "You're here!"

Morlun raised a hand without looking at Traveller.

"It is I, Judas Traveller," he said, approaching the giant villain. "I have awoken you, the greatest evil, back to your proper plane of existence. I summon you in the hopes that I may serve you, that I may be granted a sliver of your power to help you rule the entire time—"

Traveller was interrupted by Morlun—who moved with a speed that belied his bulk and size. Before Miguel could really notice, the pale villain had Traveller by the throat and was lifting him up above them all.

"Silence," Morlun said, his fingers tightening around Traveller's throat. Miguel could hear the gray-haired villain wheezing in response. "How I came to live again is not relevant. You are not relevant. I need energy. I hunger."

Miguel watched as the woman tried to struggle to her feet. He watched as Morlun, still hoisting Traveller up in the air, looked at her.

"You . . . Ghost-Spider . . . Gwen Stacy," he said, baring his teeth. "You will do."

The kick happened before Miguel knew he was launching it, but it still felt late. Either way, it landed—hard—knocking Morlun back a few paces. He dropped Traveller and righted himself. Miguel landed a few feet away—alert and ready for whatever was next. He was tired of watching. Waiting. Listening to villains prattle at each other. If they had any shot of stopping Morlun, it was now—while he was weak, and while Miguel and this so-called Ghost-Spider had some momentum.

"You dare?" Morlun said, rubbing his jaw, red eyes glaring at Miguel.

Ghost-Spider stood next to Miguel. They shared a brief glance before turning back to Morlun and the now-standing Traveller.

Ghost-Spider spoke.

"I sure do."

CHAPTER 31

The roar was deafening—and scary as hell, Miguel thought. He leapt out of the way, barely dodging Morlun's gigantic fist as it smashed into the roof of Empire State University. Ghost-Spider went the other way.

They looked at each other as Morlun tried to pull his hand out of the rubble.

"You got a plan?" Miguel asked.

"Nope, you?"

"Nada," he said, jumping at Morlun and landing a few quick punches to his face. Before the ageless villain could respond, Miguel had done a backflip to create distance between them.

"You notice he seems to be getting . . . bigger?" Ghost-Spider said as she shot a few strands of webbing at Morlun, distracting him momentarily. "Like, the more that giant brick over there glows and spits out energy, the stronger he becomes?"

"That is . . . a problem," Miguel said, sending another kick into Morlun's midsection. He felt a shock of pain shoot through him. It was as if Morlun himself had turned to stone. "He's getting tougher, too."

"Of course I am, fools," Morlun said, swatting Miguel away, catching him unawares for a brief moment. "I awoke in a fragile state, but that was not to last. The longer I stand here, the longer I collect your misplaced power from El Obelisco, the smaller your chance of survival becomes."

Miguel landed a few feet away, disoriented and feeling a strange ache spreading through his body. Morlun meant business, and the more time passed, the less likely Miguel and Ghost-Spider were to have any shot at stopping the guy.

They needed help.

Miguel pulled himself up, his legs wobbly, his vision blurry. He watched as Morlun stomped toward Ghost-Spider, that sick, creepy grin still plastered on his face. He started to move toward them when he felt an arm wrap around his neck. He tried to pull away but was overpowered.

Traveller.

"Now, now, Miguel, we mustn't press too hard," the villain said, his breathing hurried, excited. Morlun had tried to crush his windpipe a few moments before, and Traveller was still in the creature's thrall. It was pathetic. "We need our ruler to grow. To reach his final, ultimate form. Then, and only then, will my plan be set."

Miguel slammed his head backward, feeling his skull crash into Traveller's face, the muted crunch of his nose breaking bringing some slight pleasure to the hero.

"Don't you get tired of hearing yourself talk, Traveller?" Miguel said, wheeling around, watching as Traveller folded into himself, his hands covering his bloodied nose. Miguel sent a kick into Traveller's midsection, launching the villain farther away. Even before he'd connected, Miguel realized he was going at Traveller too hard. Ever since he'd regained his powers, Miguel had held back, knowing his strength was not meant to be unleashed on mortal men. While Traveller was anything but mortal, the sound he heard when his foot connected with the villain was a sign that he'd used a bit too much force.

Miguel watched as the gray-haired meddler slid toward El Obelisco, slamming into the giant artifact with a soft *thud*. Miguel saw Traveller slide down and plop on the floor next to the massive device. Miguel didn't have much time to savor the hit, though.

He heard a yelp and turned to see Ghost-Spider in Morlun's grip, the monstrous creature's pillar-like arms clutching the hero. Morlun looked down, not at

Miguel, but at Traveller—who had managed to right himself and head for the vampiric villain. From his vantage point, Miguel could see Morlun smile.

"Traveller, you are persistent," he said with a gruff laugh. "How sad."

"You owe me, Morlun," Traveller said, his voice a crackled whine. "I brought you here and—"

"I owe you *nothing*," Morlun said before dropping a giant knee onto Traveller. The shriek of surprise and pain that followed would haunt Miguel for the rest of his days. When Morlun got up, Ghost-Spider still in his free hand, the man that was Judas Traveller had been reduced to a twitching, crumpled heap. Miguel had to squint to ensure the villain was still alive. A slight twitch of Traveller's arm confirmed that he was. Miguel had to get Ghost-Spider out of Morlun's grasp—fast. He shot a web line above Morlun, but the gray-skinned monolith intercepted, holding Ghost-Spider with his other hand.

Then he pulled.

Miguel couldn't react in time, and next thing he knew, he was hurtling through the air—with Morlun's fist on the other side.

Thwack.

Everything seemed to go black for a second, then crackle into existence again. Miguel was on the ground, his skull throbbing—blood in his mouth. He couldn't see clearly—but he saw enough. Morlun, a foot raised over Miguel, Ghost-Spider in his other hand. Morlun was about to squash him like the proverbial bug he was.

So much for saving the universe, huh? Miguel thought.

Then things *really* went black.

CHAPTER 32

How is this possible?"

Gilberto's words seemed to hang between the three of them—Anya, her papi, and . . . her mami. Or a very good facsimile.

"Sofia?" Gilberto stepped toward the woman who'd appeared to Anya just a few moments before. She opened her arms, welcoming him into a tight embrace. "¿Cómo es posible?"

Gilberto pulled back, hands on Sofia's shoulders. Anya scanned her face. The woman looked like her mother. Had aged enough to be her mother now. Was it true?

"It's me, Gilberto," Sofia said, smiling, tears streaming down her face. "I'm home. I found my way to you."

"Where'd you go?" Anya said. The novelty had worn off. Now she wanted facts. Where had her mami been all this time, if she was, in fact, standing right in front of her? "What happened to you?"

Sofia hesitated. Gilberto placed himself between Anya and Sofia.

"Arañita, you have to give your mami a minute, okay? She's been through a lot, I imagine. Let's give her some time—"

"Papi, you're a reporter—this is what you do. Drill down for info. Don't let this cloud you," Anya said. She motioned to the television, which was set to the local news. A bubbly reporter was announcing sightings of various time-lost villains across the city, culminating in a large battle atop Empire State University. "The world has gone nuts. This could be part of that."

Sofia bristled.

"Anya, it's me—what else can I say? I am back. I—"

"What was the song you used to sing me to sleep?"

"What?" Sofia asked, giving Anya a confused look. "What does that have to do with anything?"

"You sang it to me every night. When Papi started singing it to me after you left, he said I'd just cry and cry, so eventually he started singing something else," Anya said, her voice shaking, her eyes reddening slightly. But with anger or sadness? Both, she thought. "So, just remind me of the song. It's an easy enough question. Right . . . *Mami*?"

Her emphasis on the last word, the tone dripping with questions and doubt, made Sofia's face contort; for a split second, at least it seemed a second to Anya, it seemed like the woman standing before her had morphed into something else. But she couldn't tell.

"I, well, I've been gone for so long, Anya," Sofia said, shaking her head. "And been through so much—I just can't . . ."

"'Cielito Lindo,'" Anya said, walking toward her room.

"What?"

"That's the song. You sang it to me every night, like clockwork. Parents don't forget that," Anya said. "At least my mami wouldn't."

She slammed the door behind her.

She could hear her papi rapping on the door gently. The sound growing in volume along with his voice, at first pleading, then concerned.

She felt her body fold, felt her knees hit the floor.

She'd wanted it to be true. Oh, how she'd wanted to embrace the lie—to jettison that lingering doubt, the one that grew and grew, eventually becoming impossible to ignore. She wanted her mami back, Anya thought. She wanted nothing more than to just fall into the deep abyss of Traveller's powers. Because the fiction—the mirage—was the closest thing Anya had experienced in years to having her mami here. To a reality she was slowly realizing could never exist. She wanted to believe, but she couldn't. That's not how her brain worked. It wasn't how her dad's did, either. She took a deep breath. Let her legs straighten out. She had to move. There was no time to lose.

Anya had other stuff to worry about now.

She saw the news report. She could spy the vampire-like bad guy—Morlun—on the roof of the school. He was alive, thanks to Traveller and El Obelisco. From what Anya could make out, Miguel was there, along with another hero. But that wouldn't be enough. And the longer El Obelisco poured energy—their own potential—into Morlun, the worse it was gonna get. Anya decided that she would deal with her "mami" later. But her gut told her if they defeated Traveller, whose power was based on creating realistic illusions, "Mami" would be long gone before Anya came back.

She slid into the last bit of her costume, then pulled the goggles over her eyes. Her room door swung open. Gilberto stood in the doorway, mouth open in shock.

"Anya . . . what?"

"I have to go, Papi," Anya said, stepping toward him—dressed as Araña. "We have a lot to talk about. And we will. But now's not the time."

Gilberto raised a hand, then paused and pulled back. He spoke softly, resigned and understanding.

"Arañita, you must think your old man is dumb, eh?" he said, a humorless scoff escaping his lips. "I knew what you were doing the second you started to do it, hija mia. I waited. I watched. I stayed up late. I prayed. But I knew the time would come when you would tell me yourself. When you'd muster up the courage to talk to me. But most of all, Anya? I was proud."

Anya felt her mouth hanging open but couldn't bring herself to close it. All this time, she'd just assumed she was the smart one. Sneaking around, climbing out of windows, evading her papi's gaze. But he wasn't just anybody—he was one of the sharpest journalists in the city. If anyone could've put it together, it was him. She just hadn't been smart enough to notice.

"You . . . you knew?"

"C'mon, Arañita, do you think I was born yesterday?" he said softly, no hint of anger in his voice. "Your patterns changed. Your habits changed. You were tired all the time. As a parent, your first thought is the worst case—drugs, relationship problems, trouble. But when I dug deeper—when I got to the truth? I was so impressed with you. You're making a difference out there."

Anya started to respond but was interrupted. Her papi pulled her into a hug, holding on to her tightly. She hugged back. She loved this man. The fact that he'd known—all along—and let her fail on her own terms . . . Anya would never forget that. She pulled back.

"I have to go, Papi."

Gilberto nodded.

"Are you . . . are you going to be okay?"

Gilberto's eyes widened, giving her a questioning look.

"With that . . . thing," Anya said, struggling to find the right words to describe the apparition pretending to be Mami. "That—"

Gilberto placed a hand on each of Anya's shoulders and crouched down slightly, to Anya's eye level.

"Don't worry about me, Arañita," Gilberto said. "Your papi may be old, but he's still sharp. As much as I wanted that . . . to be true. As much as I wanted to see your mami again . . ."

He stopped himself. Anya could see his mouth closing, his lips holding back the words as his eyes tried to hold back the tears. She hadn't seen her papi cry in so long. But the tears were always for the same reason. His partner was gone. She placed a hand on her papi's face and looked into his eyes.

"That's not Mami," Anya said, motioning toward the woman—or apparition—standing in their living room, watching them. "We have to accept that."

"It's not, niña. You were right," Gilberto said, shaking his head gently, a tear streaking down his worn face. "I wanted to believe it. So much. But it's not."

She hugged him again, quickly this time, before stepping around and confronting "Sofia."

"Whoever you are, I want you to know one thing: I'm coming for your boss," Anya said, shooting a strand of webbing that wrapped itself around the woman. "Sofia" struggled, her face morphing into something dark and monstrous. "This ends tonight."

"Nothing ends, Anya," the creature formerly known as Sofia growled. She looked more like a nightmare than her mami now, Anya realized—long fangs, red eyes, her skin gray and lifeless. "And you're headed to your doom, just as Traveller foretold."

The creature seemed to melt—or fade—into nothingness, leaving an empty space where "Sofia" once stood. Anya felt a sharp pang of sadness. She'd figured out the truth pretty fast, she knew. But it still hurt. For a brief moment, the void that her mother had left had been filled—by hope. By the chaos of the universe. Somehow, her mami had come home and wanted to be with them again.

She clenched her hands into fists.

But it wasn't real. It was just a trick by the main

trickster himself, Traveller. A manipulator who'd just awoken a timeless monster that could rip the fabric of time apart.

Anya looked at the news, ignoring the tears streaming down her face. Tears cried for a woman she hadn't seen in years.

The news ticker said it all—*MASSIVE SUPER-HERO BRAWL ATOP ESU.*

She saw Miguel, valiantly attacking Morlun as— according to the news—Ghost-Spider tried to hit the vampiric monster from another side. But Anya knew they were losing. She could see it. They needed her.

"I have to go, Papi," she said, her eyes still on the screen. The skies around the battle seemed electrified— orange-and-green lightning bursting through the clouds. This was bad.

"I know," Gilberto said. "I'm proud of you."

She turned around and smiled at her papi.

"I'll be back, okay?" she said. She didn't really believe her words herself, but she had to say them. He nodded. Not because he had nothing to say, but because he couldn't form the words.

"I have to go be a hero."

She hugged him one last time, harder than ever before—taking in the moment, imprinting it onto her memory. The truth of the matter was very different, Anya realized. She didn't think she'd be back. The odds were stacked against them. But heroism wasn't about fighting the battles you knew you'd win.

It was about fighting to win no matter what.

CHAPTER 33

The broken figure crawled toward El Obelisco. Fingernails pulling it forward. Both its legs broken. Bloody and bruised. The pain unlike anything he'd ever felt. This was the end, he thought. But it didn't have to be.

He felt his fingertips digging into the shattered asphalt that surrounded the ancient relic. Felt his elbows pop as he tried to position himself—to sit, his back to the giant device, the reason this was all happening.

Judas Traveller was dying. He was not a fan. He was also angry.

At himself, mostly. He'd been wrong. He was rarely wrong. He'd spent years—moving the pieces into play, removing others from the board—trying to set the stage for Morlun's rebirth. He realized early on that he could redirect the energies of these Spider-Heroes. He could then absorb the potential they lost—the lives saved, the heroic acts, the "good" of it all—and use it. But he had to do the work. Like a surgeon slicing carefully into someone's midsection, he picked the moments with great care. Destroying that Spider-Man from the future's life, killing his brother and erasing his fiancée. Removing Araña's mentor—and her mother—from reality. And pecking away at the main Spider, Peter Parker, as much as he could. With each step, with each jab, he gained potential, and potential was power—until, finally, he'd stored up enough to allow him to transfer it into El Obelisco, an artifact so old and loaded with power and totemic energies, Traveller almost couldn't believe his luck.

Once he had the device under control, Traveller figured the next step would be easy—drain the remaining energies of the already-fragile Araña, then summon Morlun. But something had gone wrong when he attacked the teen—sending her hurtling into the future and only taking a piece of her abilities, and not all of her potential. It'd derailed Traveller's plans, forcing him back into the future, a trip that proved more perilous with the artifact in tow. But he'd had no choice. Araña's trip into the future had thrown everything into chaos again. Traveller could see that much. She was a wild card, and he didn't like wild cards.

It was all the girl's fault, he thought as he tried to catch his breath. He looked across the stretch of battered concrete and watched as Morlun manhandled the two helpless heroes. Traveller felt a brief pang of guilt—*he* had unleashed this monster. He had miscalculated and destroyed his own plans, thinking that he could somehow control the timeless power of a creature like Morlun. But he would have figured that out on his own, had his initial plan just *worked*. Instead, Anya had ruined it all.

No matter, he thought, straining to stand, his hands holding on to El Obelisco for support. A man as wise as Judas Traveller always had fail-safes. Backup plans. He just hadn't expected that things would come to this. Not so quickly.

Judas Traveller gripped the artifact with more intent, muttering a chant as the device's ancient energies began to pulse with more urgency—and move. No longer flowing into Morlun, replenishing the monster, but toward Traveller himself.

"I am, if anything, a vengeful man, Morlun," Traveller said, resting his head on El Obelisco, feeling the energies surge through him. "And I will not be felled so easily . . ."

CHAPTER 34

Miguel looked dead. He was curled up in a ball, his body next to Morlun's foot.

The other hero, Ghost-Spider, wasn't doing too hot, either, Anya thought. This was bad. Real bad.

She'd come as fast as she could—but she couldn't help but feel like she was already late. The entire roof was in a shambles, and El Obelisco was lit up like a pinball machine, with that long-haired weirdo Traveller holding on to it like his life depended on it. What was he doing? She didn't have time to worry about it.

She focused in on Morlun, fast and hard, a kick connecting with the monster's jaw. It seemed to surprise him, knocking him back a few steps—but not much else. Anya landed near Miguel—she thought she heard him say something. She braced herself, giving Morlun her most defiant glare.

"So, you're the big, bad Spider-killin' vamp, huh?" she said. "Not impressed."

If Morlun ever smiled, she expected him to crack up now—but instead the giant, tanklike villain frowned.

The way you'd frown when a bug got in your water, or you spilled your coffee on the street. A minor annoyance that would be forgotten in short order.

"Araña, the middling spider-girl looking for a place in this wide, complex spider-world," Morlun said, his voice low and booming. She felt her hands start to shake. Not from his voice. From fear. "Do you think you stand a chance against Morlun, when your friends have fallen like pawns? Why even bother?"

"Because we can!"

The yell was followed by a series of punches that throttled the villain, sending Morlun stumbling and spinning. Anya watched as the woman known as Ghost-Spider pummeled their foe, but even she could tell it was a last burst of effort rather than something the hero could sustain. Still, it was working—Morlun, despite his bluster, was far from invincible.

"You think we just got these duds, you *Twilight* reject?" Ghost-Spider said, facing off against Morlun, who was straining to stand up. "We're heroes. And we're not just going to roll over and let you win. So, let's cut the boastfest and get down to it, okay?"

Something was wrong, Anya thought. Morlun was supposed to be some kind of impossible-to-beat power, some top-flight Big Bad. But here he was, acting like he had a nasty hangover.

And where did Miguel go?

She didn't have time to find him. She rushed at
Morlun, setting her shoulder and slamming into the
bad guy's back, feeling some of the pressure give in a
way it hadn't before. She thought she heard him moan
in pain, too.

Anya watched as Ghost-Spider took a cue from her
and went high with her next attack, sending a boot
into Morlun's face. The blue-and-gray behemoth spun
around and landed on his back, a low moan escaping
his mouth. He seemed out of sorts, confused. Morlun
was not used to losing. But *why* was he losing?

Anya looked over at El Obelisco and got part of
an answer—she saw Traveller, who had seemed broken
when she got on the scene, looking pretty amped up,
the artifact's powers and energies seeming to course
through him. Was that it? she wondered. Had the time-
traveling manipulator shifted the stream of power to
himself instead of to Morlun?

And where the hell was Miguel?

She got her full answer before she finished the
thought.

CHAPTER 35

What are you doing?" Miguel yelled, his voice lost beneath the strange sounds now coming from El Obelisco. He watched as Traveller seemed to spasm, the energies from the giant artifact pulsing through the older man, his eyes white with power, the orange-and-green light show dancing around him. He was angry, Miguel realized—and that was dangerous for the entire universe. "You'll destroy us all!"

"If that is the price the universe must pay, so be it, Miguel O'Hara," Traveller said, though he didn't bother to turn around to face his foe. "You see, El Obelisco is a transmitter—one created before man was even protoplasm. I spent years researching it—sifting through the myths and legends to find the truth. To discover that this device, originally created in ancient Lemuria, had somehow found its way up to the land, to Cuba—to be celebrated as just another old hunk of metal and stone people didn't understand. But I knew. I knew the potential behind it. It would be mine. But it is much more than what you fools think. Pure power has arrived."

Traveller started laughing—a low, frightening growl. Miguel watched as the villain—who before had seemed on the brink of death—was now blistering with power, looking decades younger, his flowing gray hair now mostly black.

Then Miguel tapped him on the shoulder.

Traveller's head spun around, looking annoyed and surprised.

"It also doesn't shut off."

"What?" Traveller snapped. "What are you even talking about?"

"See, this is your problem, Judas—may I call you Judas?" Miguel said, feeling the ache that seemed to cover every inch of his body. But he pressed on. "You think we're just fools in tights, hopping around to make your life a little bit harder. But we're not. We're much more than that. In fact, I'd like to think I'm pretty good at this whole 'science' thing. And from your future, no less. So, when Araña showed up and started talking to me about El Obelisco, I did a little digging. Then I did a little more when I got here, to your time."

"What's your point, imbecile?"

"There's no proof of El Obelisco powering anyone up. It's never been used for what you're trying. So . . .

my point is, old pal, that all this energy you're absorbing?" Miguel said, motioning toward El Obelisco, which was now shaking violently, the pure power churning through it, disrupting its equilibrium. "It's not meant to give you power. It's meant to destroy you completely."

Realization flashed across Traveller's face, then rage. It felt like Miguel was witnessing the entire spectrum of emotions in less than a second. But Miguel could tell Traveller knew he was right, even if he wouldn't admit it just yet.

"No . . . no . . . not now . . . so close to my final victory," Traveller said, stepping back from the giant artifact. But the power no longer needed him to be touching the device in order to transfer—it seemed to leap onto him, sending shock waves of energy through him.

Traveller turned around, enraged. He was ignoring Miguel. He had another target in mind now.

Miguel watched as Traveller sprinted toward Morlun, screaming with every step.

"Oops," Miguel said.

"No, no . . . it cannot be."

Anya watched as Morlun stumbled away from them, watching his hands. From what she could tell, the giant, pale villain was literally crumbling before her eyes. But why? She didn't have time to mull it over. She raced after Morlun and sent a barrage of quick one-two punches into his back. He spun around, and Anya gasped at the sight.

This wasn't Morlun. Not anymore. Once tanklike and robust, this creature was melting before her eyes. His face sagging. Eyes drooping. Mouth hanging open. Not to mention the fact that he was literally *falling apart*.

Ghost-Spider ran up beside her.

"What the hell is going on with him?"

"Not sure, but it's good for us, right?" Anya asked before sending another kick into Morlun. Her foot seemed to squish when it connected, whereas before it'd felt like she was kicking steel or concrete. Morlun howled in pain. "I think whatever brought him back . . . stopped?"

"Basically, but that's not our big problem now." Anya watched as Miguel ran over, his arms pointing toward another figure darting toward them. It was Traveller. Sort of? The aging baddie looked like he'd spent a year at a spa retreat—fit, wrinkle-free, and newly dyed. Plus, he was really, really mad. "This guy is."

The three heroes took a few steps back as the jacked-up Traveller took a massive swing at the thing that looked more like a messy lump of protoplasm than the once-fearsome Morlun.

"You *dare* betray me? Judas Traveller? After all I sacrificed to bring you here?" Traveller screamed as his fists cut through Morlun, shredding the villain to dust, leaving a pile of debris around the now-all-powerful Traveller. "But that was my mistake—I should have sought the truth for myself, as I am the one true nexus of evil."

"Wow, he's really chugging the Kool-Aid, huh?" Ghost-Spider said. She had to speak loudly, though, because a strange humming sound was permeating the air around the heroes.

"He's in for a rude awakening," Miguel said. He started to say something else, but was interrupted by a chirp. He looked at his wrist, and Lyla appeared, looking concerned. "What is it? Kind of busy right now."

"This struck me as pressing, Miguel," Lyla said with a playful shrug. "According to my readings, we're getting some major time abnormalities . . . emanating from wherever you are, focused on that gigantic power conductor."

"El Obelisco?"

"Sure, that sounds right," Lyla said, a blank smile on her face. Sometimes Miguel had to remind himself that Lyla was a holographic assistant, not his only friend. Or was she both? "Whatever it's called—it's not really . . . that stable anymore? It seems like it's had to send a lot of energy, then pull it back and . . . send it elsewhere?"

"What does that mean, Lyla?" Miguel said. Anya could hear the panic in his voice. This was not good.

"It means, Miguel, that if that object blows up, it'll tear a rift through the timestream so large that, well, we won't be able to repair it," Lyla said, frowning. "The universe will, in effect, cease to exist."

"No pressure, huh," Miguel said.

"Well, no more than usual," Lyla said with a smile.

"Uh, yeah, that's, like . . . the definition of bad," Ghost-Spider said, looking over Miguel's shoulder. "So, what do we do? Can you ask your genie?"

Before Miguel could comply, Lyla fizzled out.

Miguel tapped at his wrist. Nothing.

"Uh, guys?" Anya said.

Ghost-Spider and Miguel turned to see what she was pointing at. It was Judas Traveller. As in, it had been Traveller. Whatever was in his place was bigger than Morlun, scarier, and probably more powerful. Gone were the gray locks and gentle grandpa veneer. In its stead was a man of maybe twenty, with long pitch-black hair, glowing red eyes, his entire body crackling with energy.

"I feel it now, coursing through every part of me," Traveller said, his voice in stereo—bigger than one person, like someone screaming through a PA system no one wanted to listen to. "The power is mine. All the potential—the lives touched, the people saved, the miracles achieved . . . all pouring into me. I can see it all. I can experience it all. I am in harmony with everything—I can be the evil I'd sought to study. I am the subject now."

"Wow, nerdiest villain motivation ever, huh?" Anya said. Even she could catch the nerves in her joke.

"This seems problematic?" Ghost-Spider said as the three heroes looked on, watching Traveller stomp down what once was Morlun. "Like, very problematic?"

"No time to debate it," Anya said, jumping up as Miguel and Ghost-Spider jumped to the left and right of Traveller, who barreled through the area like a runaway train. He looked energized—more than just younger—he looked vibrant and reborn. But Anya also noticed the powers and energies coming from El Obelisco weren't stopping. Even now, fully powered, the device was shaking, and Traveller seemed a bit concerned.

She landed next to him.

"You know you're on borrowed time, right?" Anya said, meeting Traveller's stare. Her eyes calm, focused—his skittish and manic. How was this once-human man dealing with the flood of powers entering his system? How could any man deal with it? "That thing," she continued, pointing at El Obelisco, "is not going to stop pumping you with power. It will never stop. And when you break—it's going to blow itself up and destroy everything around us. Is that what you want?"

Traveller spat out his response.

"Let it," he said. "Destroy it all, I don't care. I have savored the power. I have done the true work. You see, little girl, it took me a minute to realize that in this journey, my journey, to discover the true secret of evil—I found it along the way. By seeing all the good you and your friends could've accomplished, I understood true evil, and it was me. I was the unseen darkness. The creature who manipulated you both to not only hurt you, but to hurt so many others you'd never save. So much more powerful than just a buffoon wearing an animal costume. I became the ultimate secret villain. How novel, eh? But instead of having this grand moment of clarity upon meeting Morlun, I now realize that I saw evil in the doing. In myself. So, if it all goes up in smoke now? So be it. I have reached my final form. I have tasted true evil. Now I can bask in the—"

Her fist landed squarely on his nose. Her knuckles hurt. He was more surprised than injured. But she had to do it.

"I let you ramble on too long, so just shut up, okay?" Anya said. "You might want to see the entire universe flushed down the toilet, but I don't—I have things I want to live for."

Traveller seemed curious, intrigued by Anya's words.

"Do you really?" he asked. "Even after . . . everything?"

She narrowed her eyes.

"Even after your mentor's untimely demise?" Traveller continued, his mouth forming a slight, sly grin. "Or your mother's . . . disappearance?"

She didn't respond in words. The sound she made was more of an animalistic growl as she leapt into the air, feet and arms whaling on the villain. He seemed to relish it—the punches and kicks and screams. By the time Anya stopped, a few moments later, almost collapsing on herself—she felt broken. Every muscle sore. Every joint bent too far. Defeated. She looked up at Traveller. Expecting to see him battered, bruised, bloody. But saw nothing. Just the same smiling face, younger now, but the same face she saw that night—when her mentor Miguel was killed. The same smiling face she saw in the church in the future. In an alley in Brooklyn. Haunting her. Menacing her. Tormenting her. *Why?*

"Don't you see, Anya? It's over," Traveller said, laughing like an impish child trying to get away with a bad deed. "Morlun or not, the evil has been unleashed—and now I get to watch the universe collapse."

Anya stumbled backward, her head spinning. She felt a tightness—in her throat, in her stomach. A sense of utter, complete defeat. Because she knew Traveller was right. He'd won. It was over. How could they come so close only to fail? she wondered.

Mami.

What had Traveller meant? Did it matter at this point?

Anya hated herself for crying. Hated the feeling of her own tears streaking down her dirty, bruised face. But what could she do? El Obelisco was going to explode after it unloaded all its power into Traveller, and then they'd all be dust . . .

Wait.

She turned around, ignoring Traveller's cackling, and caught sight of Miguel, huddled next to Ghost-Spider, both watching as El Obelisco continued to sputter and shake, its last surge of power escaping slowly.

She grabbed Miguel's hand; he turned to look at her.

"We need to reverse it," Anya said, out of breath.

"Reverse it?" Miguel asked. "The artifact?"

"Yes, we need it to start pulling the power back, from Traveller. Can we do that?"

"Uh, I would say no, since this is an ancient artifact that we're not exactly familiar with—"

Ghost-Spider tapped Miguel's wrist.

"Try your genie again—maybe your Wi-Fi's back."

Lyla fizzled into existence—but her presence was interrupted by static and the image was blurry. Still, she was there. For now.

"Miguel—you're okay, that's good to see," she said, smiling. "Did you save the day?"

"Not quite, Lyla," Miguel said. "Can you sift through any of the research on El Obelisco to see if there's a way to . . . reverse the polarity on it?"

"What, like what Traveller did?" Ghost-Spider asked.

"Not exactly," Anya said. She glanced at Traveller— the villain was standing in the middle of the ESU roof, hands raised to the sky, shaking at the onslaught of

energy streaming at him. "Traveller shifted the stream
of potential—from Morlun to himself. We want to turn
it backward."

"But then the overload is still a problem, right?"
Ghost-Spider asked. "We still need to figure out what
to do with the artifact?"

Miguel's wrist buzzed. Lyla spoke.

"The bright side, from what I can tell, is that if you
do somehow flip the polarity on El Obelisco, it won't
shred the timestream to bits," Lyla started to say.

"That's great," Anya interjected.

"But it will explode and destroy everything within
a radius equal to the distance between Antarctica and
Havana," Lyla finished.

"Not great," Anya said.

"But still better," Miguel said, looking at Anya, giving her a quick nod of approval, before turning back to
Lyla. "So, how do we do that, Lyla? How—"

They were interrupted by an anguished cry—a
bloodcurdling scream unlike anything Anya had ever
heard. And it was coming from someone who'd once,
long ago, been a man. A mutant who could make illusions. But who now wielded the power of a godling.

Traveller was bigger, taller, broader—like a statue
of himself. Stronger, but slower. Each step crushing
the cement below his feet. He didn't even seem to blink

as he lumbered toward them, crackling with orange-and-green energies. The heroes lined up next to each other—super-hero instinct, Anya thought. Even the green ones knew how to brace for the Big Battle.

"It needs a conduit," Lyla said, interrupting Anya's dire thoughts. "It can't just suck the power back—it needs to send it somewhere else, or at least funnel it through someone else, apparently."

Anya heard Lyla's words and knew what she had to do.

"Then we're sunk," Miguel said, not noticing Anya stepping back. "There's no way we can do that. Whoever does it is dead."

"We're all dead if someone doesn't," Ghost-Spider said, looking at Miguel and the mini Lyla. "And we're probably dead if we try to—"

Traveller struck, slamming both hands into the ground in front of Miguel and Ghost-Spider, sending them spiraling in different directions. They both recovered quickly, but the strike was just the beginning—a signal to the heroes that Traveller was here, and he was ready to rumble with them. The once-loquacious villain had gone completely silent, now just stalking Miguel and Ghost-Spider, like a cat who's spotted a mouse cowering in the corner. It was frightening.

Miguel jumped toward him. If this was the end, so

be it, he thought. He'd lived a good life. Been a hero.
Returned to being a hero, too. Thanks to— Wait, he
realized.

Where is Anya?

The fist slammed into his body before he could
get a good look around him, and Miguel felt his body
being hurled across the roof. He hadn't had time to
brace or loosen his body to lessen the impact. He got
hit hard, far, and good. Everything ached and stung
before he landed, his body scraping on the jagged
cement of the roof, stopping just inches from the edge.
He took a moment to remember he was still alive, then
lifted his head. He'd expected to see Traveller towering
over him, arms raised for the killing blow. Instead,
he watched as Traveller and Ghost-Spider tussled,
the younger woman hopping and darting around
him, dodging his sweeping, clumsy strikes. But each
one seemed to get closer, as the power-mad mutant
assimilated Ghost-Spider's tricks and methods. It was
only a matter of time before he landed a hit and sent
Ghost-Spider into orbit.

Miguel tried to get up, but a sharp pain shot through
him—spreading all over. He wasn't sure if anything
was broken. He just . . . couldn't . . . get up . . . yet.
But then a flicker of light caught his eye, and his heart
sank.

He saw her, next to the giant artifact, a tiny figure—a bug in front of an SUV. She was glowing now, too. Miguel didn't need an explanation. He knew exactly what was going on.

Anya was going to sacrifice herself.

CHAPTER 36

Anya wasn't sure how, but she knew what to do. She could feel her body vibrating as she got closer to El Obelisco. Felt that nauseous feeling again, the signal that her powers were going to fade. Except now the feeling lingered, and her powers were still intact. Almost as if her body sensed it was getting closer to the source—closer to completing what had started when Traveller first blasted her with this infernal device.

She placed her hands on the smooth surface of El Obelisco, and for a brief moment, the artifact stopped shaking—almost like it was noticing her, recognizing her; then it started again. But the frequency was different, faster, more urgent.

Anya didn't feel anything at first. Just warmth from her hands. But then she realized that warmth *was* what she was supposed to feel—and it spread, a tingling sensation, like she'd get when she'd sleep on her arm for too long, or sit cross-legged on her bedroom floor. Little pincers poking at every inch of her body. Individually annoying, cumulatively painful. She wanted to scream, but even inside her mouth that feeling remained, the sense that every inch of her body—every cell inside her—was electrified.

She opened her mouth to scream, but no sound came. She felt herself shaking violently now, as the light show around El Obelisco intensified and . . . moved. Over to her. On her. Around her. She wasn't just watching the lights go off, or reacting to the artifact anymore, she was in it—she felt everything at once and was feeling more and more as time passed. She saw it all.

She saw Judas Traveller, the older, gray-haired version that she'd first met, plotting and planning—tormenting Miguel O'Hara's brother, Gabriel, haunting a woman who had to be Dana, Miguel's fiancée. Lurking in the shadows. Making promises. Disrupting. Menacing. Destroying. Then she saw Traveller—that night, when her mentor, Miguel Legar, died, except now she could *really* see him. Watched Traveller order the attack. Saw him cackling as the Sisterhood of the Wasp destroyed the only teacher Anya had ever known. But then she was somewhere else. Another time. Her apartment. But different. It was like seeing a memory, pulled from her brain, except it cut through the haze and sepia-toned filter and brought her to that moment.

Anya could see herself, only a few years old, being ushered into her room. Could see, through someone else's eyes, as her father—looking so much younger—waved good-bye as he headed to work. It was late. She felt herself—or the body she was in—walking into her father's bedroom. *No.* Heading toward the dresser. *No, please no.* Turning to face the mirror. *Don't be . . . don't be her.*

She saw her mother looking back at her. She was in her mother's body. She was looking at herself.

And Judas Traveller was standing right behind her, a dangerous, terrible smile on his face.

She recognized the clothes her mother wore. The expression on her face. She recognized it all, because it was a powerful, lasting memory for Anya.

It was the last time she'd seen her.

Anya screamed again. This time she could hear it. Could feel the scream slashing through everything. Could feel the power not only channeling through her, but being expelled—being sent out around her, like giant waves of energy. She could *see* it, even though she knew her eyes were closed. The orange-green energies slamming into Traveller's new form, spinning him around. Could she will the powers to create a bubble around Ghost-Spider and Miguel, dear Miguel?

She opened her eyes—could see everything in what felt like hypertime, color trails following everything as it moved. Anya could sense everything around her, it felt like. Could hear a bird's wings flapping a half mile away. She turned around. She looked down at her hands, glowing with the power that had come from El Obelisco. Felt the power inside her. She lifted her arm toward her friends. Pointed her finger at Traveller, who was looking at her with the strangest expression on his now-slightly-older face.

It was fear.

Judas Traveller, for what may have been the first time in his life, was afraid.

Anya laughed.

"Whoa."

Miguel nodded as Ghost-Spider said the word. This was a big "whoa."

"That was a bad idea," Miguel said.

"What do you mean?" Ghost-Spider asked.

"She's diverted the flow of power from El Obelisco to Traveller, but now it's flowing through her—it could destroy her," he said, his voice cracking slightly. "She's bought us a few minutes—but at what cost?"

"She put her life on the line to give us a fighting chance—we can't miss our shot," Ghost-Spider said as she jump-kicked Traveller.

Miguel followed, sending a combination of punches into Traveller's midsection, feeling more of a response now than before—Traveller seemed vulnerable all of a sudden, if not fully human. Miguel heard him groan as Ghost-Spider landed another kick to his face. Their united assault pushing Traveller back. Miguel dared to look up and saw something akin to steam coming off Traveller, but colorful, orange and green like the power pulsing from El Obelisco. Was Traveller shedding power now, his connection to the artifact severed? Miguel couldn't know for sure. But he liked to think so.

"This is not the end," Traveller hissed, swatting at Miguel, landing a glancing blow on his chin and sending him reeling backward. He then turned and grabbed Ghost-Spider by her white hoodie, spinning her around and tossing her a few feet from Miguel. "You think I worked this hard to be defeated by three second-rate Spider-knockoffs? Not again. Not today."

Miguel heard a rumbling sound—like little explosions happening under his feet. He dodged another swing from Traveller—slower, less focused this time— and turned toward the noise. What he saw shook him. It was Anya—still in her Araña costume, but different somehow. She had an aura, Miguel thought, an energy field surrounding her. Unlike Traveller when he'd gotten souped up by the device, she was still Anya—not younger, or bigger, or different. But she was energized, and she was heading their way.

"Stand down, Traveller," Anya said. She sounded confident and empowered. Traveller dropped Ghost-Spider and seemed to forget Miguel was nearby, turning his entire body toward Anya. "This ends now."

"Does it, girl?" Traveller asked. "Do you really think so? Did you think I'd just allow it all to slip away from me so easily?"

The worry Miguel had seen cross Traveller's face was gone now, replaced by a manic desperation that frightened him. The look of someone with nothing to lose, and little time left.

"You've made a grievous error," Traveller said, eyes wide. "To think that I, Judas Traveller, didn't have one last trick up my sleeve."

Traveller was screaming now as he stepped toward Anya. Though the older man had been weakened, he was still strong, and Miguel had no idea how powered-up Anya had gotten. He guessed this was as close to even as these things came. But what was Traveller hinting at?

Then, as if in response to his thought, Miguel saw it. They were everywhere. Surrounding Anya. Travellers—dozens of them, in every shape and size.

Older ones. Young ones. Tall ones. Angry ones. Pow-erful ones. Miguel locked eyes with Anya and could see—could feel, even—her panic.

Then they charged.

Each variation of Traveller ran toward Anya, each scream at a slightly different pitch, creating a tidal wave of manic sound that was unlike anything Miguel had ever heard. Like an angry, murderous mob howl-ing in deadly unison.

CHAPTER 37

Anya wasn't going to freak out. She couldn't.

Everything depended on her.

She swatted the first Traveller away—older, slower, but closer. He yowled as he slammed into a younger, fitter version of himself. Both were slow in getting up. This was just a dent, though, Anya realized. There were over a dozen of these Travellers—and they were all focused on bringing her down and reaching El Obelisco. But then what?

Somehow, Traveller had tapped into the timestream and pulled himself out of every possible path this story could take or had taken. That was Anya's guess. That meant she wasn't just facing off against the Traveller that had made their lives miserable, but alternate versions that either did worse or better. Some that might've stalled out in a different time. One or two that didn't get that much power from the artifact during this, the climactic battle, and perhaps a few that never started this journey to begin with.

That made Anya wonder something.

"Hey, Spider-Man," Anya shouted over the pack of Travellers, motioning for Miguel. She smashed two of the Travellers—one clean-shaven and white-haired, the other young and kind of cute if Anya was being honest—into each other. They slid to the ground, but she knew it was only momentary. Miguel swung on a web and landed by her side as Anya completed her sentence. "Got an idea."

"All ears, Araña," Miguel said. Anya caught a glimpse of Ghost-Spider taking her rear—protecting her open flank. They were all surrounded now. But they were together.

"If Traveller pulled out all these versions of himself . . . did he pull them out from the same moment in time? Is that possible?"

"Not really my area of expertise, but I'd guess that would be challenging—while there are a number, perhaps an infinite number of iterations of each second or decision, I doubt he has the ability to just snatch different versions of himself from a single moment," Miguel said, ducking to avoid a punch from a large, energy-juiced Traveller. "So, my guess is each of these guys is from a different moment in time, perhaps close to us in terms of time, or timeline proximity."

"So, these are slight deviations from the, uh, main Traveller," Anya said, tossing Ghost-Spider into a crowd of Travellers and watching her knock a few down with a sweeping kick and a quip. Anya still felt powerful—the artifact's energies were still pulsing through her. The tattoo on her arm was vibrating at a rate higher than she'd ever experienced. But it just didn't seem to be enough. She—they—couldn't defeat a baker's dozen of Travellers. Not when they'd had so much trouble with just one.

"Sounds about right," Miguel said before taking a punch to the gut from one of the more wily Travellers. They were holding their own, but for how long?

"Do you see now? There's no escaping us—me," the Travellers said in unison. The effect was haunting. Like a swarm heading their way. "The more energy you expend, the closer we will be to the device—and to final control."

Then the laughing began, unified, echoed laughter, bouncing across the roof, ringing in their ears.

One of the Travellers leapt at Anya, grabbing her throat. She shook him off, watched as the villain slammed into the ground. She felt her fingers grow hot, orange-and-green energies crackling from her palms; her first instinct was to pull back, but she felt a voice inside her—a familiar one—speak. Her soft words hovering in her mind.

Let go, Arañita.

She did. The energy blast left her hands quickly, and by the time it reached Traveller, the duplicate villain was already fading, his scream muted by the gradual disappearance of his form. Somehow, Anya knew he wasn't dead. That wasn't how this worked. He'd been sent back, somewhere. Sent back different.

She looked at her hands. Anya Corazon knew what to do now.

She leaned down, her mouth next to Miguel's ear.

"Watch my back, okay?" she said. Miguel nodded. He was in pain. The guy hadn't worn the costume in years, and in less than a day he'd been pounded and kicked and tossed around like a ratty doll. She gripped his shoulder and smiled. "Wish me luck."

"You got it," Miguel said.

She watched him motion for Ghost-Spider to take a trio of approaching Travellers. Anya could see their new friend was at the brink, too. Her costume was in tatters. She was favoring her right leg. They were a mess. It was time to end this.

Anya prayed she was right.

She'd only have one shot.

She could feel El Obelisco humming as she got closer, the noise rising as the artifact's vibration intensified.

Everyone wanted this power. Wanted this energy. Traveller was desperate for it. A path to reanimating

Morlun. To destroying the timestream. To breaking, twisting. Even Anya felt a desire to clutch and manipulate now that the power was inside her. But she also knew El Obelisco was just a means to an end, a way to collect power and divert it. She also knew there was a limit—only so much anyone could take. She'd proven that just now, by using her own power to blast that one errant Traveller away. But what if she—

"No, no, no, little one," Traveller—the main Traveller—said, wrapping an arm around Anya's neck. "Now what do we think we're doing here? Trying to disrupt my—"

She didn't hesitate, flipping Traveller forward, his back crashing into the Empire State University roof—hard. He moaned on contact but got to his feet fast. Anya needed him out of the way for this to work. But she'd go through him if she had to. Kind of preferred it, to be honest.

"Your sick game is over, dude," she said. She felt herself powering up. Felt the energies revving, moving to her hands—preparing to be expelled. She thought she caught Traveller glancing down, too. Noticing what was to come. "You think you can just mess . . . with us? With our lives? Because you have some twisted jones for the dark side? For looking at what's messed up and terrible in the world? Well, that's—well, that's really just sad, okay? I don't even know you, man, and you've taken my teacher away—hurt my friends, my family. For what? Because you like to see what evil does? Well, now you get to see something else . . ."

Traveller opened his mouth to respond, but Anya didn't give him a chance.

"Take a look at what the good guys can do," she said.

Then she cut loose—and for a split second, everything went white, the light blinding her.

She felt the energies pouring out of her, blasting through Traveller, then past him after he'd faded away—like a river bursting through a broken dam, the waves of energy crashing into the artifact. By the time her vision returned, she could see El Obelisco not just shaking but manifesting massive tremors as she doused it with the power she'd been gifted. The orange-and-green light taking on a brighter, lighter hue—a high-pitched sound coming from the core of the device.

A few moments later, she could see more cracks beginning to form, the device's smooth surface now cobwebbed with lines, the entire artifact shuddering so much Anya worried it'd tip over—but she also knew, in her heart, that it wouldn't.

Then she collapsed. Traveller was gone, and she

felt a great emptiness. The power inside her was gone, too. The power she'd gained from El Obelisco. She felt depleted. Exhausted. But had she made a mistake? She turned to see Miguel and Ghost-Spider still battling what was left of the horde of Travellers—had she miscalculated? Had that voice—*Mami?*—been wrong, too?

The noise again. The high-pitched wail. Louder. Higher now. She looked back to see El Obelisco not only glowing, but *bursting* with energy, waves of it coming out in concentrated blasts—strong, focused beams. She followed them with her eyes—watched as each one intercepted a Traveller. Within minutes, they, too, were faded and gone. Leaving Anya, Miguel, and Ghost-Spider standing on the roof of the building.

They turned to face each other. Even with their masks on, Anya could tell Miguel and Ghost-Spider were smiling.

"Did that just happen?" Anya asked.

"You did it, girl," Ghost-Spider said, giving Anya a thumbs-up. "Way to go."

Anya tried to talk, but couldn't. The sound wouldn't come. She couldn't believe it.

Had they really won?

She felt the tears start to roll down her face. Just as she felt the floor beneath her start to shake.

Anya spun around. El Obelisco was there—still

shaking, but even worse now. Shaking so hard that the ground around it was shattering, shrapnel and shards of concrete flying around. The energy didn't just pulse around it—it seemed to throb, like a bubble or balloon prepping to burst. It wasn't blasting energy out anymore. That's when it hit Anya. It hadn't just faded the Travellers away to where they once were—the artifact had absorbed them, and all their energies and powers, in addition to all the power she'd blasted back into the ancient device.

"Oh no," she said.

Miguel raced toward her, stopping a few feet from the artifact.

"This is not good," he said. Anya watched as Lyla flickered into existence—well, the small version.

"Miguel, what is going on? Are you back yet? I miss—"

"Lyla, no—it's what you mentioned. This thing is gonna blow," Miguel said, frantically waving his wrist toward El Obelisco.

"Oh, that's not ideal," Lyla said, her tone unchanging, as if she were discussing a grocery list. "I was hoping it wouldn't explode."

"What?" Anya said.

"Yeah, it's overloaded—too much stuff happening, plus . . . it looks a little bloated?" Lyla said.

"Bloated?" Ghost-Spider asked.

"Did I stutter?" Lyla said. She brought up a bigger display, a holographic image of the device—but as part of a bigger schematic, showing energy moving in and out like a flowchart. "This thing is *old*, Miguel. You knew that. It can only take so much. Did . . . well, did any of you send more energy into it? More than it had inside before?"

"I did," Anya said, her voice meek. She thought it'd been the perfect idea, but had she just gone on impulse rather than strategy? "I just thought . . ."

"Don't beat yourself up," Miguel said, waving her off. "You saved the damn universe, Araña."

"Well, to be technical, the planet is still very much in peril—" Lyla said.

"Quit it, Lyla. Helpful words only," Miguel said. Anya could tell he was tense. The artifact was starting to crack—larger fissures pushing through the smaller ones. It was falling apart before their eyes—and Anya had no idea what that meant beyond, well, boom. "What do we need to do?"

"Get rid of it—it's a temporal disturbance, but it only seems to work when it can affect people," Lyla said, showing them another schematic of El Obelisco—a cloud signifying the range of its power growing slowly, each step ratcheting up Anya's anxiety. "It seems like the powers would dissipate, though, if it's far enough from—"

Miguel tapped his wrist, and Lyla disappeared. Anya watched as he straightened up.

He walked over to the device, which was crackling with more power now, the structure itself barely visible beneath the light show it was giving off. Miguel crouched down, sliding his hands under El Obelisco, the giant device tilting slightly. He was strong, Anya knew. But not *that* strong. She watched him struggle and strain.

The device shuddered again—this time Anya heard a loud, deep cracking sound.

They were a minute, maybe two, away from total destruction.

CHAPTER 38

He can't do this.

The words pounded in his skull. Over and over.

You're old. You're not Spider-Man anymore. You're not even the real Spider-Man.

Just give up.

Miguel pushed past it. Pushed past the doubts. Not because he wanted to, not because he'd had some kind of awakening about himself—but because he had to. Had to save Anya, Ghost-Spider, Lyla, everyone. This device, this infernal piece of ancient stone, was going to destroy everything. He couldn't allow that.

So, he strained. He tried to lift it. Maybe if he was able to generate enough momentum, he could clear the skyline and minimize the damage. Maybe.

He could feel the ticking clock. Each second one step closer to oblivion.

How had it come to this? he wondered. Why was it resting on his shoulders? He wasn't a hero. Not anymore. Traveller had taken that from him. Had taken his brother. His future wife. His entire life.

Miguel groaned with the strain, only able to tilt the huge hunk of metal and rock slightly. They were doomed.

But then there was something else.

Movement. The object was rising. Miguel looked to his left.

Anya.

She was lifting it, too—and pulling some power from the device itself, keeping it level, staving off complete destruction for a few more moments.

"No, Anya, don't—this could kill you," Miguel said, trying to hold up his side of the artifact. "I need to do this. I need to take care of it."

"This could kill you, too," Anya said. "Let me help you. Sometimes being a hero is about working together."

Miguel smiled under his mask.

"Who's the veteran now, eh?"

Anya winced as she lifted the device over her head. She and Miguel were holding it up, but it was back to shaking violently, the cracks growing deeper. They wouldn't be able to hold it much longer.

"I've absorbed a bit of the power, so I think . . ."

Anya said, the strain on her face evident. "I can toss this up, with a little help."

"You got it, sis," Ghost-Spider said, coming in on the open side, giving them each a slight bit of relief. "But then what?"

"Then you guys toss this thing up high and fast— and I hold on and guide it away," Miguel said. He kept it brief. He knew the pushback would come.

"What? Why? You'll get— You'll die," Anya said, as if realizing Miguel's fate as she spoke the words.

He'd die.

Miguel was strangely okay with this. He'd done his part. Been the hero. He'd been resigned, just a few days before, to living out the rest of his days as just . . . Miguel. Alone. Working at Alchemax. The desire to put on the tights and do some good had been destroyed— by a time-traveling villain hell-bent on exploring the true depths of evil. But that was done. He put on the suit again. He helped save the day.

Now he had to save the world.

"Lyla," Miguel said, unable to tap his wrist. Holding up a giant obelisk will do that to you.

"Hi, Miguel—you seem busy."

"This is probably it."

" 'It'?"

"The end, Lyla," Miguel said. He didn't feel any shame hearing his voice crack. He loved Lyla, holo-assistant or not. "I need to steer this ticking bomb away from New York. Away from people."

"By doing that, Miguel, you will not have ample time to remove yourself from the explo—"

"I know," he said. "I'm calling to say good-bye."

"Oh," Lyla said. Her smile was gone. Miguel knew holo-assistants weren't built to emote or to have human reactions beyond their programming. But he also knew Lyla was special. He knew there was something in there. If not a soul, then something like one. "I am not prepared to release you from our friendship, Miguel."

"It'll be okay, Lyla," Miguel said, with a dry chuckle. "You were a better CEO than I was. Just pretend I'm alive and run the show?"

"Like *Weekend at Bernie's 3000*? Dubious, but I will take it into consideration," Lyla said, rubbing her chin. "But, Miguel—do know this: You are a great man. You will not be forgotten."

"Thank you," Miguel said. It was all he could manage to say. He closed his eyes tightly. When he opened them again, Lyla was gone. He looked at Anya and Ghost-Spider, both holding other sides of the giant, collapsing artifact.

"Let's do this."

CHAPTER 39

Anya felt the power coming back through her—somehow the device was able to use her as a conduit, like it'd used Traveller. She felt stronger. She also felt the urge not to stop. To just get more powerful. To be the strongest. She heard the voice whispering inside her head. But it wasn't a good voice. It was not the path Anya wanted. She just wanted to go home, hug her papi, and sleep for a week.

But the damn world needed saving.

So, she took just enough power—felt her strength increase a dozen times over. She was lifting El Obelisco on her own now, her fingers getting singed by the orange-and-green energies crackling off the surface. Ghost-Spider and Miguel had stepped back, watching carefully as their young friend hefted something akin to a giant dinosaur above her head as if it were a small pillow.

Ghost-Spider looked at Miguel.

"You got this, Spider," she said. "You're gonna save the damn world."

"Last chance," Anya said. "You can still change your mind."

"No time," Miguel said, jumping on El Obelisco, part of him lost in the glare of the energy. She could tell he was in pain, even through the mask and lights. This would not be easy. "Just toss it hard and long, kid. I'll do the rest."

Anya nodded. She started to pull back but stopped.

"Mig—Spider-Man, I just wanted to say something," she stammered.

Miguel raised a hand.

"No need," he said, the words falling out hastily, like someone in a rush to get offstage. He couldn't handle saying any more. "You're a hero, Araña. If you think I taught you anything, just know you taught me so much more. You reminded me what it was like . . . to be a hero. Why it's important. You gotta keep carrying that on after I'm gone, all right?"

Anya opened her mouth to respond but couldn't.

"Now let's go," Miguel said.

Anya finally spoke.

"I need you to stay," she said, realizing this tiny, whimpering voice was hers, but she didn't care. "I need a teacher. We can get rid of this together, okay? Just let me think."

"You don't. Not anymore," Miguel said, almost

fully consumed by the lights and energies, his voice distant and pained. "You've learned everything I can teach. Keep helping people. Keep fighting."

Anya nodded.

She pulled her arms back, moving the giant object. With a scream of pain, rage, and anguish, she and Ghost-Spider sent El Obelisco—along with Miguel O'Hara, Spider-Man of the year 2099—hurtling into the sky.

Ghost-Spider stood next to Anya as they watched the bright, inflamed object grow smaller, until it was a speck of darkness on a bright, New York afternoon. They watched as the device continued to fly up into the sky—the speck becoming smaller and smaller. Then, suddenly, a gigantic burst of orange-and-green energies enveloped the skies—spreading out like a spilled cup of water on a table. The flash was brief, disappearing a moment later.

Anya and Ghost-Spider looked at each other. Looked around the roof. The damage from the battle had disappeared. They were alive.

But Miguel was gone.

Ghost-Spider pulled Anya in for a tight hug.

"He saved us all," Ghost-Spider whispered into Anya's ear. "He saved us all."

CHAPTER 40

Anya's shoulders sagged as she stepped toward her apartment door. It was late in the evening. She felt exhausted. No, not just tired—she felt deflated, almost dead. Every inch of her ached, inside and out. Like she'd gone twelve rounds with all of the heavyweight champs, back-to-back. And, if she thought about it—that's exactly what just happened.

But it was more than a physical ache. She felt broken inside. Losing Miguel—another Miguel, but still hers—was something she didn't expect to hurt this much. A familiar emptiness enveloped her, but it felt stronger now. Despite her best efforts, Anya was doomed to be alone in this hero biz. She was forever meant to be navigating it blindly. How much longer could she do it? she wondered. How much longer before she ran into something she just wasn't ready for?

She fumbled through the pockets of her civilian clothes and muttered under her breath. She'd forgotten her keys. On any normal day, it'd be nothing—an annoyance, something trivial to shrug off. But not today. She felt the tears streaming down her face. Felt herself crumpling to the floor. *Why?* she wondered. Why couldn't the world just give her one, tiny—

Break?

She felt the door open, her body weight shifting forward.

Anya looked up, expecting to see her papi, looking down, concern enveloping his face. But she saw someone else. Someone she never expected to see again. At least not after what just happened. But she was here. For real this time.

Sofia Corazon looked down, her eyes as tear-lined as Anya's.

"Anya . . . it's me," she said, her voice a cracked whisper. "I'm home."

———

And so she was.

Except this time, it wasn't an apparition created by Traveller—it was actually Sofia Corazon, Anya's mother, gone for over a decade. She was older, too—but still the mami Anya remembered.

"I feel like I was just here," Sofia said, her voice soft and nostalgic but also scared. "Carrying you around, singing you our song . . ."

She hummed a few bars of "Cielito Lindo," and

as she listened to the song, whatever doubts Anya had were gone. What remained was confusion and wonder.

Sofia led Anya into the apartment's small living room, and Anya saw her papi, sitting on their tattered couch, hands folded in his lap as their eyes met. His expression was clear: *This is real. Mami is back.*

"But . . . how?" Anya blurted out, before even taking a seat. Sofia tried to take her hand, but Anya pulled back reflexively. This was too much. Everything was too much. A few hours ago, she'd been in this room facing off against an unnatural aberration, a trick. But this was not that—Anya just *felt* it.

"How are you here?" Anya said, turning to face Sofia, then looking at her papi. He motioned to his newly alive wife to speak. Anya watched Sofia, her mami, take in a long breath.

"Anya, I—I wish I had an answer," she said, shaking her head, more to herself than anyone else. "But . . . the last thing I remember was being here, with you, with Gil—and then walking out, looking for that man, Traveller. After that I remember . . . nothing. A void. Darkness. Like I was walking through smoke and fog, for what felt like . . . it was endless. And then I was here, in this apartment again. Except everything was different. Like I'd slept through my entire life."

Now it was Sofia's turn to cry, her sobs racked and

heaving. Anya stepped forward, pulling this woman, this mother she'd thought gone forever, into her arms. She felt Mami's head rest on her shoulder, the tears pouring onto her, the muffled cries echoing into her ear.

"How?" Anya said to herself, seconds before she felt her papi embrace them both. His wife back, his daughter home.

Anya pieced the truth together slowly, over hours—sitting with Mami, their fingers woven together. Through the tears and laughter. Through a hesitant meal. The ice melted quickly, pushing through the disbelief and confusion to a fragile acceptance.

Somehow, Anya figured, Judas Traveller had absconded with Sofia Corazon, transporting her to some kind of pocket world, where time moved differently—where hours were actually years. Years stolen from Anya, years meant to weaken her hold on being a hero, years before she even gained her powers, even decided to become Araña.

"Mami, I still don't get it—because we just . . . we just fought Traveller," Anya said. The secrets had fizzled quickly, too. Soon, Sofia knew what Gilberto had done—that their daughter wasn't just much older, she was a freakin' super hero. One that had just been ensnared in the biggest battle of her life. "And he was powerful, sure—like, reality-altering stuff . . . but to be able to hide you for years? How is that—"

"He . . . he wasn't alone. He'd been haunting me, hounding me—and I wanted to find the truth, find out what was going on. So I left our home, and I confronted him. But he just laughed, and the next thing I knew, I was somewhere else—in that fog," Sofia said haltingly. "Then there was someone else, there was a woman, she said she was part of a group, the Sisterhood—"

"Sisterhood of the Wasp?" Anya said.

"You've heard of them?" her papi asked, desperate to be a part of the truth, the reporter in him unable to just sit back and listen.

"Yes, they're some kind of ancient organization, hell-bent on destroying the Spider Society, the group Miguel Legar—well, my old mentor—was part of," Anya said. She watched as her mami nodded slowly. "The Sisterhood seemed to disappear, though, when Miguel Legar died."

"The woman, Charlissa, appeared to me—regularly," Sofia said. "She would taunt me. She called herself the All-Mother, the leader of the group. From what I could tell, my capture was a product of their black magicks, but it was not something she could do alone. She said . . . I forget exactly, but she said someone had 'helped her,' had 'added to the Sisterhood's power.'"

"Traveller," Anya said. "He must've found a way to augment the Sisterhood's spell, because they could take you away—they could hurt me and maybe prevent me from becoming a hero."

That's when Anya felt it all crashing down. Felt the dark reality of what this man had done to her come into full view. Not only had he caused the death of Miguel Legar, her mentor, and Miguel O'Hara, the Spider-Man of the future, but he'd also manipulated the Sisterhood of the Wasp into concocting an evil spell to hide her mother away—all in the hopes of breaking Anya's spirit. All so he could steal away her potential to resuscitate an eons-old vampire in Morlun. If it wasn't so tragic, Anya thought, she would laugh.

She felt a hand fall over hers. Anya looked up and saw her mother's eyes.

"I'm home now, mija," Sofia said softly. "And I will never leave you again."

CHAPTER 41

She woke up with a start. Anya saw the sun sneaking in through the blinds of her room. It was time to get up. Time to head to school. Time to pretend like everything was fine and normal.

Except it wasn't.

Though it'd been a few weeks since she sent her friend flying into the sky on a suicide mission, it could've been yesterday. So much had changed, and though life was prone to straining to return to routine and normalcy, she still felt a thick hangover from the fight. Traveller's interference didn't just fade away—but some things did return to their rightful place.

She rubbed her eyes and hopped out of her bed. She scanned the room. She could see pieces of her costume strewn on the floor, clues about the night before. She still felt achy and tired. But Araña and Anya were not the same person—at least not to the outside world, so she didn't have an excuse to be late for class. She also had a responsibility to protect her neighborhood.

She felt the tattoo on her arm pulsing slightly. She

touched it and got a brief sense of relief. Ever since the battle with Traveller atop ESU, her powers had stuck around—some kind of residual effect from El Obelisco's potential-loaded energies coursing through her. Too long, didn't read: Anya's powers weren't on the fritz anymore. If anything, she was slightly more powerful.

Anya opened her bedroom door, hoping to make a quick beeline to the bathroom to shower. No such luck.

"Long night?"

Gilberto's expression was kind and understanding, but Anya couldn't avoid seeing the sting of worry in his eyes, too.

She nodded sleepily.

"Who was it this time?"

"Oh, some weird-ass dude in a scorpion suit, of all things," Anya said with a shrug. "He was teaming up with another guy—the Spot?—to rob a few banks. It was easy."

"Doesn't look like you had it easy," Gilberto said.

Anya gave him a wry smile. He was right, as usual.

"You take them down, though?" he asked.

"You know it."

Gilberto smiled. She could see the concern morph into pride on his face. It made her feel secure. She wasn't hiding anything anymore, and having her dad in her corner meant so much. She turned to head into the bathroom, but her father stopped her with a slight pat on the shoulder.

"Arañita, are you really going to start your day without saying hello to Mami?"

Anya turned to face her father, a warm smile on her face.

"Mami?"

Sofia watched as Anya entered their small kitchen, a warm cafecito in her hand. She was in a robe, looking mostly rested.

"Arañita, did you sleep well?"

"Not really," Anya said with a shrug. "But you know the drill."

Sofia smiled.

"I know you were careful."

"Pretty much, Mami," Anya said, stepping around her mother to open the fridge and pull out some milk. "How are you feeling?"

"I'm tired, but happy to be back," Sofia said, looking pensively at her coffee. "It felt like an instant to me, yet somehow, much time has passed. So much has changed. It will take some getting used to."

Anya nodded. She wasn't sure how to process what had happened over the last few weeks, but it all shifted forever that night—after Miguel's death. She'd walked through the front door of her apartment to find her papi standing in the living room, a look of pure shock on his face. Anya couldn't shake the vision of Sofia— Mami. Looking older—looking the way she should look now, after so much time. She'd been confused, she told them. She was back after what, to her, seemed like no time at all. She'd left that one day to try to fig- ure out the truth about what had been happening to her. The mysterious man who had been tracking her, haunting her. And she'd found him—confronted him. But then darkness. When she woke up, she was back where she'd seen him, except everything around her had changed. The city was different. And now—her little girl was a woman. Her husband was older, too. They all were.

It was a process.

But Anya knew the woman she was seeing was her mami. Knew she was real.

Most importantly, she knew why now, too.

"Time travel is weird," Spider-Man had told her. The original Spider-Man. He'd reached out to her after the incident with Traveller, mostly to thank her and Ghost-Spider for saving the day—but also to check on Anya. He'd met them atop the tennis stadium in Forest Hills, Queens. The meeting felt casual but important, like Anya had finally been brought into an inner circle she knew existed but had yet to join. When she told him what happened, he seemed to understand—and to share her pain. As much as anyone could when you're celebrating the return of a relative you thought dead and mourning the time lost.

"Based on what I learned from Reed and Doc Strange—well, Traveller mucked with the timestream a lot, hopping around and trying to nudge Spider-peeps into quitting so he could harness their lost potential. But when you drained the powers from all of those alt Travellers, you basically pulled them out of their places in time, before they could really do the damage that, I guess, Alpha Traveller needed," Spider-Man said. "So, things like your mother, or your mentor—they may not have happened the way Traveller had planned."

He'd been right. At least about her mami. Sofia Corazon was back, and it *was* her, and Anya was going to take that for what it was and enjoy it as much as she could.

Because dammit, she deserved to smile a little bit, right?

She thought of her mentor, Miguel Legar. She wondered if he was back, too—lurking somewhere, waiting to present himself. Perhaps soon. Anya could only hope. It was nice to be able to hope again.

It was also nice to be less alone.

"You did good, great even," Spider-Man had said, a moment before shooting one of his own webs toward Manhattan. "You both did. I know Ghosty understands this, but I want you to know, too—if you need help, I'm not hard to find."

"Usually," Ghost-Spider said with a snicker.

"Hey, Secret Wars only happen every few years, okay?" Spider-Man said, a tinge of insecurity in his voice. "Give a guy a break, will you? And—hang in there, Araña. You're one of us. Spiders look out for each other."

Anya smiled as she watched Spider-Man swing away. The vision lingered with her that morning, too, as she followed her mami through their tiny apartment.

"Oh, Anya, I forgot to tell you," Sofia said, walking to the end of the kitchen and sorting through a pile of mail. "This came for you—a postcard, of all things. Papi says it's a friend of yours?"

"Was it Lynn?" Anya responded quickly. "I think she's studying abroad this summer. Guess she finally got around to—"

"No, no, this is from a man—a police officer?"

Anya's heart stopped for a moment.

She ran to Sofia and snatched the card away. She looked at the address.

MIGUEL O'HARA
NYPD SPECIAL CRIMES UNIT
LYLA DIVISION

She smiled. A tear slid down her face.

"Arañita—¿qué te pasa? Are you okay?"

She looked up. At her mami's dark brown eyes. The look of concern and care she never thought she'd see again, then she looked down again at the postcard. From a man she'd grown to look up to but also thought she'd lost forever.

Sometimes the world was okay, she thought.

Anya,

I'll keep it brief and vague because, well, that's how it works in our business, huh?

I'm okay.

Somehow, I'm okay.

Thanks to you. We did it. You did it.

Keep swinging. See you sometime . . . in the future.

Abrazos,

Miguel

"Who is this Miguel, Arañita?" Sofia said, reading over her shoulder. " 'Keep swinging'? ¿Qué policía dice eso?"

"He's not really a cop, Mami—he's from the future. He, uh, he helped me. A lot, and . . . and I thought he was gone," Anya said, turning around and giving her mom a hug. A long, tight hug. The kind that was meant to make up for lost time.

"I love you, Mami."

"I love you, too, mi arañita. I love you, too."

EPILOGUE

Anya took a long sip of her iced tea. It was late morning on a Saturday, and she was letting herself enjoy the moment. Maybe she was even letting herself relax. After everything that had happened, she reasoned, she deserved that much, right?

Despite her mami having been gone for years—despite the hole in her and her father's hearts being covered by pain and time—she'd returned and taken her place as if she'd never left. Like she'd just been on an extended vacation and was ready to step back into things. Well, that wasn't totally true. The time between Judas Traveller's capture of Sofia and the second she reappeared was fuzzy, almost blank—but she was home. They could work on the rest, Anya reasoned. But for now—today—Anya was going to take a minute to herself. Maybe.

Anya heard the backpack landing on the tiny table in front of her before she saw it.

Maybe not.

"You sulking?"

Anya looked up to see Gwen Stacy, she of the back-pack, looking down at her—a wide grin on her face.

"What? Me? No," Anya stammered. "I'm just—I dunno . . ."

"Breathing? It's okay to breathe, we all need to," Gwen said, taking the empty seat across from Anya. "Glad I found you, though."

The coffee shop was empty, one of those places that felt like a chain but maybe wasn't. Kitschy art, Top 40 songs playing on the sound system, and coffee that could be described as anything but "strong." Still, Anya liked the place, and it was definitely quiet. Most of the time.

She stiffened at Gwen's comment.

"You were looking for me?"

Gwen raised an eyebrow.

"Uh, yeah," she said with a smirk. "I'm checking on you, dude. We just saved the freaking planet. Maybe even the universe. That kind of stuff . . . lingers, you know?"

Anya nodded fast. It made sense. But it made her a little edgy. She'd wanted to be alone. To think. To breathe. Or to wallow? She wasn't sure. Even with her mom back, even with Traveller and Morlun gone, she still felt a pain—an aching that she was having trouble pinpointing. Part of her didn't want to figure it out, either.

Gwen rapped her fingers on the lacquer tabletop. Her expression softer now.

"You miss him, huh?"

It took Anya a second to realize who she was talking about. The only person she *could be* talking about.

Anya looked down at her hands. She felt her body let out a long, jagged sigh. She felt the warmth on her face. Ashamed at first, she tried to fight it—but then realized she couldn't, as the tears began to collect around her eyes. She couldn't make a sound, only able to respond with a quick nod.

Before Anya could do anything else, Gwen had stood up and walked over to her, leaning down and embracing her in a tight hug. Anya could feel Gwen's face buried in her neck, her arms pulling her in. In a moment, she was crying. Hard.

"It's okay," Gwen said, gently patting Anya's shoulder. "You gotta talk about this stuff . . . and let it out."

After a few moments, Anya pulled back, wiping away at the tears and collecting herself. Gwen took her seat and reached out a hand, patting Anya's gently.

"I just . . . I'm having trouble accepting that he's . . .

well, not gone, but not here—if that makes sense," Anya said, her voice still cracking but stronger now. "I had a teacher before—also named Miguel, weird, right?—and he's dead. Now this Miguel—just as we're starting to work together, or even like each other, just as I feel like I'm learning from him—he's gone, too. I'm alone at this again. Like, I dunno if I can do this—just stumble along and hope to eventually—"

Before Anya could finish, Gwen spoke, her voice forceful.

"You are not alone, girl," she said, leaning forward, her eyes on Anya's. "Hear me, loud and clear—you are not alone. Miguel was great, and he went out a true hero. He did what we were all ready to do if it had to be done. That's what heroes do. But you're not on an island, all right? Not anymore. You're one of us."

"One of . . . what?" Anya asked.

Gwen smiled.

"This thing we do? The whole 'saving lives at the expense of our own lives'?" she said. "You're not the only one doing it. You were working in your own little silo, here in Brooklyn. I know some of us saw you a bit, but we didn't *see* you. That's on us. But you did great out there, okay? You saved the freakin' world. How insane is that?"

Anya smiled. The tears were still wet on her face, but she felt a lightness she didn't know was missing. She felt like she was part of something now.

"Is there, like, uh—a handshake?" she asked. "Or membership dues? Who else is in this? I mean, obviously Spider-Man, but, like, which Spider-Girl? Is Spider-Woman alive? What about that pig—"

Gwen raised her hands, eyes wide.

"Anya, relax," she said with a quick laugh. "It's not like a *team* team. We don't have an underground headquarters or fly around in a Spider-Plane. Helping each other—wherever we are. Heck, I'm from another *universe*. But we're around. Like a network, really. If someone comes for you, they come for all of us. Spidey himself said as much when we talked to him. You just need to start believing it."

"That's . . . that's great," Anya said, almost as much to herself as to Gwen. "I've been doing this for a while, and it's felt so . . ."

"Lonely?" Gwen said. "Yeah, trust me—I get that. And it's never not going to be hard. But you have people to talk to—people who've done this and will hopefully be doing this for a long time. We can help you become the best hero you can be."

Anya looked up at Gwen. She wanted to believe this woman. She wanted to know there was something more protecting her than just herself. People who understood what she was going through and would help her navigate what's next. Could this be it?

"Promise?" Anya asked. She hated the way her voice cracked with the question.

"Promise?" Gwen asked. "I guarantee it. Welcome to the big leagues, Anya Corazon. It's a new day for Araña."

—

"Good morning, Miguel," Lyla said, crackling into existence in front of Miguel's wide desk on the top floor of Alchemax HQ. He was not surprised to see her. This was their routine. At least it had been for the last few weeks. Since the incident. "I've cleared your schedule today."

"Oh?" Miguel responded, looking up from his datapad. "What now?"

"It appears that Thanatos has returned," Lyla said, shaking her head. "And he seems very upset."

"Is that so?"

"Yes, one would assume it's a job for our friendly neighbor—"

"Don't do it."

"Everyone's favorite web-swing—"

"Lyla."

"The amazing arach—"

"I get it, Lyla," Miguel said, standing up and walking around his desk, loosening his tie. "Can you let Gabri and Dana know I won't be joining them for lunch?"

"I think they'll understand you're . . . otherwise entangled," she said with a giggle. "Get it?"

Miguel, now fully suited up as Spider-Man, tilted his head, as if to say "Seriously?" He did have to admit—Lyla had been acting . . . strange lately. Almost human. He'd have to look into that. Again. But now wasn't the time—and Lyla's behavior certainly wasn't the strangest thing that had happened to him of late.

"I just don't want them to think I'm . . . brushing them off," Miguel said. He thought he caught Lyla giving him a warm smile—one that said "You *have* changed." But he might be projecting. Projecting on a holographic projection. He chuckled. It was nice to have some humor back in his life. Everything felt lighter after you stared death square in the eyes.

When Anya had tossed El Obelisco—and him, riding shotgun—into the sky, Miguel had just expected to disappear, to get blasted out of existence. But as the speeding artifact twisted away from Earth, thanks to his attempts to steer, Miguel started to feel something different—like he was being torn away from the very fabric of reality. For a brief moment, he saw everything—felt every emotional peak and valley of his life, caught glimpses of every major beat: his birth, his childhood, gaining powers, falling in love with Dana, his brother's death, his own darkness. It was like a shock to his very soul, and he felt himself screaming, pushing against what had happened, like some kind of mental reflex, rejecting what Traveller had done to destroy those he loved.

Then everything went white, and Miguel stopped—well, being. Thinking, breathing, existing. But instead of an endless void, he woke up in his apartment. In his own bed. But it was different. When he rolled over, he didn't find an empty space—he found Dana, curled up with an arm under her pillow, like always, muttering to herself in her sleep. He didn't believe it at first. Wanted to jump out of bed and run to fight whatever new trick or trap Traveller had set for him. But before he could say anything, something buzzed. A call.

He'd spun around and accepted it—and a dead man appeared on the other side of the holo-screen.

"Hey, bro—bad time?"

Gabri. His brother. He was alive.

Gabriel was alive.

"Gab . . . Gabri?" Miguel asked, leaning into the viewscreen, his eyes watering. "It's you."

"'Course it's me, Mig," he said, looking shaken.

"Who else would call you this early? On a weekend no less?"

Gabriel moved his head, as if trying to look around Miguel.

"Bad time?" he asked playfully.

Miguel turned around. He looked at Dana, asleep in bed, looking so peaceful and rested. If this was a trick, he never wanted it to end. He looked at Gabriel.

"It's Dana . . . She's here."

"Well, I'd hope so. If it was someone else, I'd ask you what's going on. You okay, Miguel? You're acting like you've seen a ghost."

Miguel remembered shaking his head no and telling Gabriel that he loved him. More importantly, he'd said as he leaned in to bring himself closer to the projection of his brother—things would be different from now on. He could be a hero, but he also had to be something else. A friend. A brother. A partner. He had to use this chance—this unexpected blessing—as a way to fix his past mistakes.

"Gabri . . ." he started, but he dared not finish what he wanted to say.

You're alive.

The memory flashed through Miguel's mind as he positioned himself on the edge of his massive office window, looking down on the Nueva York skyline.

The city needed him. He was up to the challenge this time. There was a lot to be done, he thought. But he'd never wanted to do it more.

"Thanatos, eh?" he asked. "Where?"

"He's tearing up downtown," Lyla said, appearing next to him on the window ledge. "Doubt any flyboys will even bother."

"Then I will," Miguel said, leaping into the open air. "Because that's what heroes do."

THE END